HEADHUNTERS

HEADHUNTERS

LUIS PAREDES

This is a work of fiction. Similarities to real people, places, or events are entirely coincidental.

HEADHUNTERS

Dedicated to my Family
And to that wonderful thief, Harvey Swick

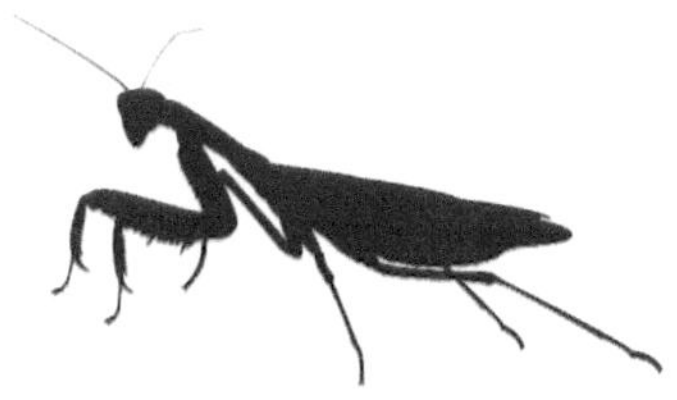

PROLOGUE

Yael Rodriguez fretted over a burbling cast-iron pot. Her cloudy hazel eyes darted between the curled yellow paper of a handwritten recipe on the counter and the stovetop.

She even checked the trash—twice—just to see if she had tossed out an important ingredient. But everything was where it was supposed to be—in the pot or at the bottom of the rubbish bin.

Yael sucked at her teeth. *¡Madre de Dios! What am I doing wrong?*

Her daughter, Christina, and six-year-old granddaughter, Isabel, were on their way, and the dinner she'd promised, Cuban black bean soup, was on the verge of failure.

Beads of sweat bloomed across Yael's wrinkled forehead as she struggled to understand why, after two hours of heavy simmering, the dark legumes were still hard as rocks.

All the other ingredients had followed their roles to a T: the meat from the ham hock had sloughed away, exposing glistening, white bone, the stinging aroma of onions and garlic filled the air, and her secret mixture of herbs and spices speckled the liquid's roiling surface like a volcanic crust.

Yael plucked a wooden spoon from the pegboard and stirred the soup until a whirlpool appeared at the center. A dull ache corkscrewed up her left arm. She stumbled backward, striking her back against the refrigerator. She slid to the floor and placed a hand over her chest. A high-pitched squeal slithered through her ears.

"Breathe, just breathe," she whispered. With her free hand, she tapped out her heart's frantic rhythm on the linoleum floor until her knuckles ached.

She heard her daughter's voice in her head, "You're eighty now, Mama. You have to take it slow." Yael rolled her eyes, but then the room started spinning.

Yael's heart slowed and the vertigo tapered away. She raked her fingers through her frizzled, gray hair, and exhaled a long, deep breath. She glanced up at the black pot and pursed her lips. *I could always order a pizza*, she thought.

The ghostly image of Yael's long-dead grandmother, Mirabel, appeared in the room; the old woman shook her head and faded away.

"Ok, Abuela. No Italian food," Yael said, laughing.

She grasped the woodblock counter and slowly pulled herself up. She cracked her back and shuffled toward the stove. Yael took a sip of the soup and closed her eyes. She rolled the thin mixture around her tongue and grunted. Something was missing. Something vital.

Then it hit her.

"¡Coño! I forgot to add the carrots!"

Yael's hand covered her mouth. If Christina had heard her curse like that in front of Isabel, she'd never hear the end of it. She dabbed her face with a cherry-red, polka dot dish towel and glanced at the stove's digital clock—four hours until her family arrived.

That was more than enough time to run to the corner store, come back, chop up the veggies, and let the carrots work their magic on the beans. She could already smell the finished dish.

If there were any leftovers, she'd take some to her neighbor, Margaret Tooms, and her young son, Edgar. Lord knows she could use the help. That boy of hers was so strange, always talking to himself.

Yael lowered the flame to the lowest setting and rushed to the front door. She slipped on her shoes, picked up her purse, and opened the door.

She screamed as a wave of cold air curled around her body and pulled her out the threshold.

———

Yael couldn't understand what had happened. The last thing she remembered was opening the front door, and then nothing, literal nothingness. The darkness spanning her vision was deeper than anything she'd ever experienced.

The black veil slowly faded and Yael found herself surrounded by pale birch trees. Their barren canopies scraped at the night sky with splayed, skeletal branches. Somewhere in the distance, a door slammed shut. The sound echoed through the vast forest.

Yael shivered. How was this possible? And why was it

so dark? It was only four in the afternoon when she stepped out the door. She glanced up and stared at an enormous moon hovering in the jet-black sky. Nothing made sense.

"Is this a dream?" she asked, not expecting anyone to hear.

Insects chittered in response. Yael covered her ears as the clicks, trills, and screeches blared through the woods. Slowly, the cacophony settled into a low buzz.

"Am I dreaming?" Yael asked again.

"No, this is not a dream," a voice gurgled.

She turned. The voice seemed to come from a small tree tucked behind a row of larger birches. Cast in shadow, the sapling swayed side to side.

"Wh-who's there?" she asked.

"My name is Andrés," the slender shape said. Two curved branches slowly unfurled from its sides like enormous jackknives. "Mrs. Rodriguez, I'm afraid you've passed away."

"This is some kind of joke, right? I'm not dead," Yael said.

"No? Why don't you look down at your feet?" Andrés suggested.

Yael glanced down and yelped like a kicked dog. She was floating several feet above the ground and her once tan skin was the color of chalk dust.

When she looked up, the shape had stalked forward. It wasn't a tree. It was a gigantic insect—a praying mantis! Yael rubbed her eyes. No! Not a bug, but a man in costume; there was a man's mouth inside the creature's head. It smiled and Yael's mind struggled to make sense of the eight-foot-tall amalgamation in front of her.

"Don't scream," Andrés said, lowering his clawed fore-limbs. The moonlight glinted off his jade-green shell. Yael saw her distorted reflection in the creature's bulbous, obsidian eyes. "Let me explain: I am a Strider. The Rookery sends me to help lost souls find their way—" Andrés twirled his right claw in the air. "—forward."

"Ay Dios mío! Ay Dios mío!" Yael trembled and hugged herself.

"It's easier if I show you," Andrés said, breathing out black smoke from between the gap in his human front teeth. The wisps congealed into a large cloud. Bursts of miniature lightning crackled as the vapor flattened. Slowly, an image of a city made of colored glass glimmered on the smooth surface.

Yael was mesmerized. The filigreed towers and castle-like structures that filled the screen calmed her. "It's so beautiful." Yael floated closer to the cloud. "It's . . . it's what I imagined it would look like."

"It's time to go, Mrs. Rodriguez," Andrés said, bowing.

"Heaven? Am I going to Heaven?" Yael asked, tears welling in her eyes.

———

Andrés smiled.

It was what he was taught to do whenever confronted with the H-word. Smile, nod, and beckon the soul forward. Luckily, Mrs. Rodriguez didn't ask too many questions; she was eager to move on.

"It's time. Please, place a hand on the cloud," Andrés said, smiling with his human mouth.

Yael nodded and touched the floating screen; the city

faded in and out of focus before vanishing completely. She gasped as cracks suddenly raced across the once smooth surface. Thick, foamy oil oozed out from the fissures. The liquid reached for Yael, twisting like living tentacles of freshly spun taffy.

She slapped a tentacle with the back of her hand; it recoiled then snapped forward, wrapping itself around Yael's arm. Slug-like nubs wriggled out from the feeler's surface and crawled across her skin. She tried sweeping them away with her free hand, but the black liquid clung to her like sap.

Yael turned toward Andrés. "Help me, please."

He shook his head and pointed toward the cloud with the tip of his claw. She turned just as hundreds of new inky tendrils sprayed out from the cracks. The plumes raced around Yael's body, weaving a glistening, black cocoon.

The casing constricted, forcing Yael into a fetal position. She hovered, whimpering. Bones snapped as the cocoon kneaded itself into a grapefruit-sized ball. Its surface shimmered with a purple haze and hardened into iridescent glass.

Andrés scuttled forward, snatched the floating orb from the air, and laughed.

CHAPTER 1
A BOY AND HIS BALLOON

Edgar Tooms stared at his grandfather's severed head and smiled.

The old man had fallen asleep by Edgar's bedside while narrating his favorite yarn: *How the Great Firefighter, Charles Tooms, Died*. It was a story told and retold over the past few years with wide-eyed theatrics and ever-evolving heroics, but never with an ending.

The cause of death—despite the title—remained a mystery thanks to his grandfather's amnesia and uncontrollable habit of passing out moments before the story's climax.

Tonight was no different, and from the sound of the snoring, there'd be no second attempt to finish the tale, denying eleven-year-old Edgar the answer to how the elder Tooms ended up as a housebound, decapitated ghost.

It was a mystery that nagged at Charles, but delighted Edgar. The cause of death didn't really matter to him; all he knew was that his grandfather's floating head, visible only to him, was special. Edgar adored Charles's thin, gray wind-swept hair, heavy-lidded eyes, ruddy cheeks, and aquiline nose.

Edgar's mother, Margaret, didn't share the same warm feelings for the father who had abandoned her when she was eleven. Edgar quickly learned that Charles Tooms was a name best left unsaid. Of course, he couldn't help it as a toddler. Edgar chuckled as he thought back to his earliest memory, the day he spoke his first words—Opa Cha.

His mother's face had turned green as those three syllables slipped out of his mouth. Cha was what Margaret called Charles when she was a child.

"How do you know that name?" she had screamed.

Edgar scrunched up his face. Years later, he could still hear the question ringing in his head; even his grandad's snoring couldn't drown out the din rattling within his skull. He shook away the noises, real and recalled, and lay down in bed. His mind always swam toward the past.

He thought of how his mother's questioning increased in frequency and intensity over the years, and how, on his sixth birthday, her approach changed, softened. That day, after all of the party guests had left, she asked him in a calm voice, "Peanut, who do you talk to when no one is around? Be honest."

The last time he admitted who he was talking to, he was shaken violently and sent to bed. He remembers stalling, but with her hand cupped warmly on his shoulder, Edgar felt like he could be honest with his mother again.

"Grandpa! Grandpa Charles," Edgar answered and gave her a full description of the old man's facial features, the sound of his gravelly voice, and personal quirks like how he sucked at his teeth when bored.

"Oh, and the skin around his eyes crinkles like aluminum foil when he smiles—like this—" Edgar had added, grinning and squeezing his green eyes shut. "Oh, and Mom, he has the same part in his hair as me. And his earlobes droop like honey hanging from a spoon!"

As he rattled off more details, his mother's skin turned white. This was the moment he realized that his ability to see Opa Chuck wasn't normal. He promised himself that day that he'd hide his ghostly interactions from his mom, other adults, and kids. Especially kids. The mean ones saddled Edgar with the nickname Tombstone Tooms.

The moniker followed him through grade school and was whispered in hushed tones as he walked through the hallways or was hollered during lunch as Edgar ate alone in the far corner of the cafeteria. The school's administrators insisted that Edgar switch to home schooling, but Margaret put her foot down and demanded her son attend classes despite the bullying.

"My husband died in Iraq, I've got a shitty nine-to-five that barely pays the bills, and, what, you want me to homeschool, Edgar? Pay for a tutor? With what money? No. He's going to school. Understand me?" He remembers her yelling into the phone at whoever at Springhurst Elementary had to deal with angry parents. He too had pleaded with his mother to stay at home, but her will won out and he went back to the cinder block house of taunting.

Edgar covered his face with his lemon-yellow sheets in a vain effort to block the memory of those elementary school days. But the scenes of humiliation and anger taunted him.

A high-pitched wheeze snapped Edgar's attention back to the present. He watched as his grandfather bobbed up and down with every sonorous breath and wondered, *How the heck does he breathe without lungs?*

Edgar shrugged off the question, crawled to the foot of the bed, and picked up his grandfather. Charles only looked solid; he could pass through most objects instantly.

To make contact, Edgar's outstretched hands had to trace the phantom contours of Charles's head like a fortune teller reading a crystal ball until an electric charge buzzed between the two. Then came the sudden presence of mass, as if a bowling ball had dropped into Edgar's palms.

The first time it happened, Edgar laughed and then vomited. His grandfather's wrinkled skin, lips, teeth, and thin, gray hair all had the unexpected—and unsettling— texture of a rubber balloon. And Charles's noggin wasn't so different from a balloon: they both floated through the air, could be squeezed out of shape, and deflated.

But with each successive *Catch*, as Edgar liked to call it, the revulsion passed. Now, the weight and feel of his grandfather's head, especially when cradled in the crook of his arm, felt comforting and empowering. Edgar thought of himself as a low-key superhero. The thoughts distracted Edgar and his grandfather's head started to lose its solidity.

"Did I finish the story this time?" Charles asked, star- tled by the transition.

"Not this time, Opa," Edgar said, regaining his grip and placing Charles on a dresser top. In the process, he accidentally knocked over a drinking glass. It shattered on the floor and Charles rolled his eyes. He knew what was coming next.

"Edgar! Why aren't you asleep?" his mother yelled, thundering up the stairs to his attic bedroom.

The door swung open and she glared at Edgar, eyeing the shattered glass on the floor and the top of the dresser where it once stood.

"How many times have I told you to be more careful? Clean this up and get to bed. Summer camp starts tomorrow!" she snapped.

"I know, Mom. I'll be more careful." He watched his mother stomp back down the stairs.

"She gets that anger from me, you know," Charles said. "Margaret was always . . . temperamental."

"Feels like Mom's always angry, Opa. I wouldn't know what to do if you weren't here." Edgar sniffed and pressed his knees to his chest. "Will I always be able to see you?"

Charles stared at the tears forming in his grandson's eyes. "I hope so. I really hope so."

Edgar nodded, turned over, and wrapped himself in a wad of blankets.

CHAPTER 2
OPA'S SECRET

Charles Tooms gazed at his sleeping grandson. What he never told Edgar—and would never tell him—was that just before Edgar was born, he had spent weeks in the house invisible to the world.

Not even his daughter could see him. He'd scream and bounce harmlessly against the walls all day long. The nights brought new terrors to his solitary life: strange, high-pitched trilling voices, muffled explosions in the distance, and an erotic moaning oozing from the murk between life and death. He almost went mad.

It wasn't until Edgar came along that another human being became aware of him. It was a relief, and he quickly put the terror of that time behind him. But thoughts of that time were always close to the surface of his mind and they breached his consciousness like slick eels whenever Edgar went to school or fell asleep. In those moments, he felt alone again and fearful that he'd disappear completely.

His grandson stirred and sloughed off the sheets.

Charles smiled and let the thoughts fade away. He bobbed back toward the dresser and closed his eyes for the night.

CHAPTER 3
DREAM OF THE UNDERWORLD

Edgar dreamed of sitting in a cavern.

Wherever he turned, glossy stalagmites bristled from the ground like crooked witch fingers. A turquoise glow, cast by bioluminescent mushrooms carpeting the dirt floor, shimmered against the rocky formations.

"Beautiful," Edgar said, shivering. Plumes of white vapor curled out from his mouth. His nostrils flared. The crisp air smelled of musk and mold.

The sound of metal squeaking turned his attention upward. High above, a gigantic water faucet hovered in the tar-black gloom, rolling and pitching.

Edgar imagined the Statue of Liberty would have such a spigot in her backyard—if giant statues had backyards. The faucet squeaked again. Its bulbous, red knob spun to the left. Then, the brass spout aligned directly over his head.

Water collected around the threaded, brass rim and fell straight down as impossibly small droplets, reminding

Edgar of cartoon ants marching down a picnic table's leg. The dollops drummed on his forehead.

Tap. Tap. Tap. Tap. Tap. Tap. Tap.

He tried looking away, but the frigid water paralyzed every muscle in his body. Someone called his name and Edgar woke with a start.

CHAPTER 4
WAKE UP CALL

Edgar rubbed the sleep out of his eyes.

The cave was a fading memory, but the tapping persisted. Edgar turned his head. The sound echoed from the attic window not as the steady drumbeat he felt in the dream, but more like the slow, random popping of corn kernels in a cast-iron pot.

Maybe hail? he thought, stumbling out of bed. He marched toward the noise clinking against the glass, half expecting to see the backyard covered in icy pellets. But there was nothing.

The early morning sun dusted the dew-covered grass with a wan amber sheen. The bushes, still draped in shadow at the far end of the backyard, rustled. Edgar opened the window and inched his head out.

Twak! A pebble smacked his forehead. Crows in the surrounding trees cawed like a laughing TV audience.

"Ha! Ten points!" came a voice from the yard.

It was Clara Diaz, Edgar's best friend and the only person who believed that he could see his grandfather's ghost. He rubbed the welt growing between his eyes. Clara doubled over and laughed.

"It's 5:30 in the morning, Clara." Edgar groaned.

"Come on, Tooms. Let's hang out before you go to camp!" Clara said, dropping a large sketchpad.

"Keep it down. You're going to wake up my mom," Edgar hissed.

Clara pulled back her thick, garnet-red hair into a ponytail. "I saw a dead deer on the street over." She reached into the side pockets of her cargo pants and clacked its contents against each other like desiccated bones. "I brought my colored pencils."

Edgar smiled. He could never resist watching her create magic on a blank page and she knew it.

"I'll be right down!" he said.

"That Clara?" Charles mumbled.

"Yup, I'm going out for a bit," Edgar said, tiptoeing down the stairs.

"Be back before breakfast, kiddo."

The stairs creaked in response.

CHAPTER 5
MARKED FOR COLLECTION

Charles floated toward the window. He watched as the children greeted each other with hugs and laughter. He hoped that their friendship would blossom into something more as they grew older.

Despite the charming scene outside, Charles's mood soured. Today, Edgar would leave for summer camp for a month—the longest stretch of time they'd been apart.

A thump downstairs turned Charles's attention away from the window. He floated down through the floorboards and popped into his daughter's room. Margaret turned over and buried her face into the pillow. She was asleep and Edgar was outside. *Nothing in the house should be making noise,* he thought.

The thumping grew louder. Something was wrong. Charles swooped down through another floor and slowly emerged from the kitchen ceiling. Now, a scratching sound came from the living room.

A raccoon. The boy left the door open again and let a raccoon in the house, Charles thought, speeding toward the noise, but found nothing out of the ordinary in the spacious TV room.

The plaster wall behind the couch suddenly cracked. Charles floated closer and watched as the outline of a circle etched itself into the wall. An unseen hand carved out the interior and chiseled a downturned triangle on each side of the circle, close to its base.

Charles turned as Edgar walked into the room.

"Opa, have you seen my Polaroid camera? We're going to take shots of this dead deer Clara found. She says we can get a great shot with the early morning light. Something about chiaroscuro."

"Come here, Edgar," Charles said, nodding toward the wall.

"Opa, why are you staring at the wall?"

"Come look. Can you see this . . . thing here?" he asked, as inch-long lines emerged from each of the triangle's down-facing tips.

Edgar nodded and ran a finger across the design and snapped his hand back.

"What's wrong?" Charles asked.

"It's not there," Edgar said, tapping the carving. "It looks like it's dug into the wall, but the surface is flat. That doesn't make sense." Edgar sat on his haunches. "Look, there's plaster dust on the floor."

The boy was right. The carving was somehow real and not real at the same time. Suddenly, a blue light emanated from the design, flared brightly, and faded from view. The wall turned smooth again and all the dust coating the wood floor disappeared.

Edgar stood and blinked. "Why are we staring at the wall?"

Charles glared at his grandson.

"Why are you looking at me like that?" Edgar asked.

"Well, we just saw the wall carve shapes into itself. It was like there was an invisible artist—"

"Oh! Clara! Clara's waiting for me," Edgar said, walking away. He turned. "When I get back, can you help me finish packing? I have to leave before lunch."

"But the wall . . ." Charles muttered.

"What about it?" Edgar said.

Charles tried holding onto the image of the etching, but it quickly evaporated. "Um, never mind. Yeah, when you get back, I'll help you pack."

CHAPTER 6
OFF TO CAMP

Charles hovered over the mounds of clothing Edgar had tossed on the living room floor. A fluffy pillow, half a dozen books, towels, a large water bottle, granola bars, and a pouch full of toiletries ringed the two weeks' worth of clothing Edgar laid out on the living room floor.

Edgar dropped his hiking boots and sneakers on the carpet. "How the heck are we going to get all of this into *that*?" He gestured toward the empty, pea-soup-green, seabag draped over the couch.

Charles grinned. "Grab the bag and step into it."

Edgar narrowed his eyes. "Are you serious?"

"Hop to it, soldier," Charles said.

Edgar stepped in and pulled the canvas up to his eyes. "Wow, it's bigger than it looks."

"Yup, now roll the fabric down until you reach your knees."

Edgar rolled down the edges of the canvas bag. "There, now what?"

"First thing's first—step out and set your hiking boots

and shoes on their sides on the bottom. See how it flattens the bottom out?"

Edgar nodded. "Mm-hmm."

"That's your base. You're going to want to put all the bulky items that you don't need right away above that."

Edgar beamed and stuffed his pillow, books, and towels into the bag.

"There you go! You got it!" Charles said.

"Thanks, Opa. I think—"

A drawer slammed shut. Edgar and Charles looked through the kitchen pass-through. Edgar's mother waved a peanut butter–coated knife in the air.

"If you weren't out with Clara this morning, we'd be ready to go. It's almost noon and we were supposed to be on the road by now." Margaret glared at her son. "Please remind me, why am *I* making this PB&J, Edgar?"

"Sorry, Mom. I'll wrap this up."

Margaret grunted and stabbed the knife into the jelly jar.

Edgar's face twisted into a scowl. He grabbed a wad of shirts and pounded them into the seabag with his fists.

"Whoa, take it easy," Charles said.

"You know I don't really want to go, right? Mom's making me," Edgar said, wiping a tear from his cheek.

"I know. Margaret's a tough nut. She means well. I mean, I would have done the same thing to her."

"Really?"

"Yeah . . . I was hard on her back then. It was a different time." Charles turned away to watch his daughter make sandwiches for the car ride. He noticed the anger roiling behind her calm exterior and shook his head. "I should've been better," he muttered.

Edgar nodded and placed the last of his clothing into the bag. The water bottle, snacks, and toiletries followed.

"Good. Now, shake the bag so all your stuff settles and cinch the top closed and you're done!" Charles said.

Edgar wrestled with the bag for a moment and managed to secure it. He let it drop on its side. It looked like a taut, green sausage. Edgar smiled and rubbed the name stenciled on the side—Sgt. Daniel Rivera.

Charles hovered close to Edgar's shoulder. "Your dad would be proud."

"Thanks, Opa," Edgar said, sitting. "Hey, did you learn how to do this when you were in the navy?"

"Yeah, in boot camp." Charles frowned. "No, that's not true. My pops taught me how to do this. He was a grunt. Fought the Nazis in Sicily. He was convinced that I'd join up one day and that I should learn the finer points of packing a seabag when I was your age. I think I still have the lumps on my head to prove it."

Edgar rubbed his hands together. "Oh. Was he a bad father?"

Charles blew out a puff of air. "He wasn't all bad. The man had a temper. I'll tell you that."

"What was your dad's name, Opa?"

"Ezekiel, but his friends called him EK. He left when I was—"

Opa's face deformed as a sandwich wrapped in aluminum passed through his head. The crinkled square landed in Edgar's lap.

"I'll meet you in the car, ok?" Margaret said, twirling her keys.

Edgar sighed. "I gotta go, Opa."

Charles nodded and floated up as his grandson stood.

Edgar slid the seabag over his shoulders and started for the door. It was time to say goodbye.

Charles bounced against Edgar's shoulder. "Be good and take care of yourself out there."

Edgar wrapped his arms around his grandfather's head and squeezed. "I will, Opa. I'm going to miss you."

Charles burrowed out of Edgar's grip and smiled. "Go on, it's time to go."

Edgar waved and walked out the door. Charles followed just past the threshold. Any further and he risked blinding headaches and deflation. If he lost shape, it'd take him an hour to fill up with whatever it was that held him together. Charles watched the car pull away and shuddered.

For the first time in over a decade, a gust of cold air slapped his face when he bobbed back into the house. Cold air and the same strange blue light he saw earlier, but this time the glow emanated from every wall and floorboard.

Was he having some kind of afterlife aneurysm? Charles blinked hard and shook his head. "Well, that didn't work," he said, watching the light grow stronger.

Charles followed the strange illumination to the living room. His eyes darted in every direction. He couldn't shake the feeling that there was someone else in the room.

CHAPTER 7
THE BEAST ARRIVES

"You don't belong here," whispered a deep, gravelly voice.

Charles zipped around the perimeter of the empty living room. No one was there. He wondered if the stress of sending Edgar off to camp had gotten to him. He shook his head.

"Little ghost, you heard me the first time," an invisible tormentor said, louder this time.

"Who's there?" Charles asked, floating toward the ceiling for a bird's-eye view.

Charles watched as indentations appeared on the plush carpet below, but what were they? The large, three-pronged footprints reminded him of dinosaur tracks left behind in dried riverbeds.

The coffee table rattled, toppling over a teacup. A cloud of black smoke exploded in the middle of the living room and a gigantic praying mantis the color of unpolished emeralds emerged. Its spiked forearms tucked against its elongated abdomen like jackknives, as translucent, veiny wings fluttered gently behind its segmented abdomen. The creature clambered over the furniture with the help of four slender legs. It stopped a few feet from Charles and looked up.

Two bulbous eyes on the sides of its triangular head scanned the ceiling; black pupils wriggled just below each dome's shimmering surface like tadpoles trapped under ice. They swirled into black dots as they locked onto Charles. The mantis swayed left and right as if a breeze had poured into the room.

"What the hell are you?" Charles gasped and drifted further into the ceiling.

The creature's thin antennae that had been gently sniffing the air burst into furious motion, drawing stiff circles in the air. What looked like sweat beaded on the green creature's rigid carapace. The liquid dribbled along the hard plates that lined its face and body. Charles gagged. The creature's armor had the look and texture of a crab shell. He hated seafood, especially crustaceans.

The mantis hissed. Steam billowed from the sides of its mouth. Its mandibles stretched open. Webs of sticky saliva clung between the sharp tips and dripped onto the carpet. The thick, horn-like blades opened further, distending with a crack that made Charles flinch. Then the plated mouth peeled backward, crinkling on itself like aluminum foil until a dark, cavernous oval sat in the middle of its grotesque face.

Charles saw a flash of pink, and for a moment, he expected to see the creature's last meal claw its way out. But from the gaping darkness, the lower half of a human face emerged. Its flattened nose, stubble, and a sharp glossy scar on its lower lip gave the impression that a boxer hid underneath the gigantic, green exoskeleton.

Charles hadn't sweat in years, and yet, beads of perspiration pooled on his phantom skin at the sight of this strange beast's second face, ringed in shadow. Was this even real? How could a human mouth sit inside a giant insect's head? The lips moved, but Charles couldn't process the words.

The creature cocked its head to the side. "Can you hear me?"

Charles didn't know where to look as the creature spoke. Its insect eyes stared at him with an alien intensity. The strange, black pupils jiggled occasionally, but conveyed neither emotion nor empathy. And the words spilling out of its human mouth didn't sync up with the lips. It was like watching and hearing a badly dubbed foreign movie.

The beast thumped its claws together. "I'm here to take you to the Rookery," the mouth said, revealing a gap-toothed smile.

Charles's eyes widened. The Rookery? The word frightened him. Wherever or whatever it was, he knew it wasn't someplace he wanted to be.

"Come now. It's a wonderful resting spot for souls like you." Black smoke billowed out of its human mouth—its breath was course, fibrous, as if hundreds of microscopic barbs rode upon every exhalation.

"Wh-what do you want?" Charles asked, turning his face as the dark vapor floated closer.

Streams of inky smoke slithered from flaring nostrils and the space between its clenched teeth. As the darkness eclipsed its head, the creature inhaled the vapors with a snort.

"You have questions." The creature slicked back its

antennae with a claw. "Fine. The Marquis's rules say I have to answer them." The beast bowed. "The name's Andrés, and I am a Strider, a caretaker of lost souls under the employ of the Rookery."

Dozens of questions floated through Charles's mind, but he could only focus on one: "What are you?"

Andrés tiptoed closer. "I am a Phantid, and once upon a time, your ancestors used to worship us as Gods. Please, come with me and I'll show you everything."

Charles knew that the creature, this Andrés, was lying. It must have sensed his hesitation, because as soon as the thought entered his head, the creature charged, darting its arms out and grabbing Charles within the crooks of its spiked claws. Charles wriggled his head, squeezing through the gaps between the sharp spikes, but the creature clenched its claws tighter, pinning Charles for a brief second until he burst from Andrés's grip with a comical squeal.

"You're making this harder than it should be," Andrés yelled, crouching down, priming itself for another lunge. But before it could launch itself at Charles, the front door opened. Predator and prey stood still as Edgar rushed into the living room.

"Opa! Camp's cancelled! I don't have to go!" Edgar shouted, peeling off his backpack and letting it slump to the floor.

The boy's smile quickly faded away as he stared up at the mantis, its head nearly touching the ten-foot ceiling. Edgar plucked some loose change from his pockets and threw the metallic mass at the creature in front of him. The coins slowed as they passed through the mantis's body and fell onto the rug.

"Impossible!" Andrés hissed. "How can you see me, boy? You're not dead!"

In a flash, Andrés skittered around Edgar and caught Charles again. "Help me!" Charles screamed as the Strider walked backward toward the chimney.

Edgar lunged forward and latched onto the claw that held his grandfather. The creature roared as Edgar's grip cracked its exoskeleton.

"A Seer! The boy's a Seer!" Andrés shouted, staring at a jagged seam oozing thin, green blood. Andrés let go of Charles and reared up on his bowed marching legs. "You little swine!" he shouted. "Look what you did to me!"

"Stay away from us!" Edgar shouted, taking hold of Charles in the crook of his left arm and reaching for a nearby lamp with his free hand.

Andrés spread his long, sinewy arms out so fast that the curved blades at the end snapped backward. The claws slowly creaked into place revealing their black-tipped spikes.

"Edgar! Why am I carrying your duffel bag," his mother said, stomping through the door. She gasped as she entered the living room.

"What did you do?!" she shouted, walking between all three combatants. Andrés skulked into the corner, threw his head back, and exhaled a thick cloud of black smoke. The knots of darkened air formed into melon-sized puffs that collected around his slender body. Once cloaked, he evaporated with an audible pop.

"What was that sound?" Margaret turned her head in every direction.

"You didn't see it?" Edgar asked.

"See what?"

"That thing. That giant praying mantis!"

"Oh my God, Edgar! You're doing it again. You're making things up. We've talked about this."

"No, it's true. That thing was after Opa—"

She threw him a look that silenced him.

"Clean this up, Edgar, and go get the rest of your gear from the car. I'm going upstairs." At the door, she looked back at Edgar, narrowed her eyes, and said, "Are you happy? You got what you wanted, didn't you?"

Edgar's chin drooped to his chest. "That's not fair, Mom," he mumbled. Charles shook his head, and Edgar took his grandfather's advice to stay quiet.

But once his mother was out of earshot, Edgar turned toward Charles: "Holy crap, Opa. What the hell was that?"

Charles glared down at his grandson. "Don't you use that street language here in this house."

"Opa! What was that . . . thing?"

Charles floated down toward the dark mark Andrés left on the carpet and sniffed the slick residue. "I don't know, but it smells like nutmeg."

Edgar shook his head and straightened up. "I saw a giant praying mantis in the living room and it looked like it was trying to eat you . . . then it disappeared in a cloud."

There was no denying the facts: a carnivorous insect with a human mouth was indeed trying to capture him. Would he have taken a bite? Charles didn't know, but he suspected the answer was yes.

"Opa? Is it still here?"

Charles didn't have an answer.

"Wait, what are you doing back? Aren't you supposed to be on your way to summer camp?"

"They shut it down. Some kind of viral infection

spread through their staff last night and no one's able to work," Edgar explained. "Mom got the text just as we got on the highway and drove straight back."

"Oh," Opa bobbed a nod.

"Maybe this has something to do with the symbol we saw last night? I just remembered how the wall carved itself," Edgar said, turning toward the wall where the etching appeared.

Charles's mind drew a blank. *What symbol?* he thought, but as he faced his grandson, the memory of the circle and triangles appeared again. "I can't believe I forgot about that! I think you're right. It can't be a coincidence."

"What do we do?" Edgar asked.

"Get Clara. We're going to need another set of eyes."

CHAPTER 8
RETREAT TO THE ROOKERY

Andrés raged within the inky, incandescent depths of the teleportation cloud as it transported him from the living realm down through the underworlds.

He sliced at the churning black gas with his scythe-shaped claws, shredding the vapor. He hissed with frustration as the murk reformed into a swirling cocoon. What he really wanted was to disembowel the boy that hurt him, and the mist was a poor substitute for flesh.

"The little swine!" Andrés screamed. He stared at the wound on his right claw. The small, human handprint stamped onto the curved edge showed no sign of healing.

Andrés cursed the day he caught sight of that floating head. Not that he could have ignored the decapitated ghost—a Strider's nervous system homed in on spirit energy, pulling hunters like Andrés toward their prey like magnets.

And it should've been an easy catch had the boy not intervened. *That wasn't a normal child*, he thought, taking small comfort in surviving an encounter with a Seer, a human gifted with powers strong enough to kill Phantids.

Andrés turned his head as shafts of sunlight punched through the smoke. Hot air and coarse sand followed, pattering against his hard carapace. He clamped his mouth parts together, covering his fragile, human mouth.

The wind whipped faster, evaporating what was left of the teleportation cloud and bringing with it the smell of jasmine, mint, and burned coffee—the familiar aromas of home.

"About time." Andrés grunted and spit at the parched, cracked earth; the black goo sizzled and turned to dust as he oriented himself.

The teleportation cloud dropped him at the edge of a high plateau overlooking the Rookery, a volcano-shaped mound rising two miles high. It was a drab, pock-marked structure the color of wet cement. Tubular flues sprouted along its rough surface, venting white smoke. Andrés's eyes followed the curlicued vapors as they snaked toward the Rookery's twisted, tapered chimney. The oval hole at the top puckered open.

BWWWAAAAM!

Andrés flinched as the shaft bellowed its first morning alarm—a colossal brass moan that reverberated for miles around.

Andrés inched closer to the plateau's edge. "And out come the suckers."

The sound of millions of fluttering wings emerged from the city of Irkalla. The ancient metropolis encircled the Rookery like an undulating palisade with its tightly packed, mud-brick buildings the shape of hexagonal columns that bristled skyward from the unforgiving desert. Sunlight blazed across the gold-coated towers and glinted off the amethyst crystals growing from their flat-topped roofs.

Striders flew out of tall, rectangular windows neatly arranged in rows of three down the face of every structure. He envied his fellow citizens. They were about to start their daily routines without a care in the worlds. Had he come home with the ghost, he would be well on his way back to his quarters for a few days of well-deserved rest. Instead, he faced punishment. The sigil he carved into the Tooms' home was still active and alerted the Rookery to his failure the moment he teleported away.

He had until the morning's fourth alarm to make his way toward the Royal Palace at the center of the Rookery and present himself to his master, the Marquis, for judgment.

Death by immolation, beheading, or a lifelong prison sentence were the three possibilities Andrés faced. The fleshy barnacle-like breathing pores lining the side of his torpedo-shaped abdomen puckered opened and closed as his anxiety mounted.

Andrés's head dropped to his neck stalk. "It's not fair."

CHAPTER 9
UNWANTED COMPANIONS

Andrés's bout of self-pity didn't last long.

Behind him, the ground shook and the air filled with dust as dozens of Striders, fresh from their hunting expeditions, burst from swirling teleportation clouds.

Most of the older hunters clutched one or two dark balls of captured souls in their spiny forelimbs; the younger Striders, however, used leather satchels to house their prizes.

A slim Strider preened in front of a growing crowd of admirers; he turned, giving the group a look at the bulges stretching the hides of two bags on its smooth, armored back, the dark leather standing out against his chartreuse carapace. The crowd thumped their claws together as the successful hunter danced.

Andrés wondered if he was ever that cocky and self-satisfied. The youngster probably still believed in the Marquis's so-called Promise—that after 100 years of servitude, hunters would be knighted and spend the rest of their days living in luxury within the Royal Palace's gilded halls.

It didn't take long for Andrés to realize that the Promise was a lie and that the so-called nobles conspired against hunters to keep them locked in their roles for life.

Andrés stared at the youngster as he bowed in front of the crowd. The young Strider's sickle-shaped claws were shorter and slimmer than his, but they'd lengthen and thicken after a few more moltings.

The Strider caught Andrés staring and scuttled over to his side.

"Isn't the Rook beautiful, brother?" he asked, extending a slender claw toward the giant mound.

Andrés shook his head. "Show some respect, fledgling. It's called the Rookery."

"I know what it's called, and I'm no fledgling. I've been hunting for five years now." He slipped the satchels off his back. The orbs chimed as he waved the trophies at Andrés. "How many did you bring back?"

The pupils in Andrés's eyes shaped themselves into flames. "What's your name?"

"Cleitus."

"Well, Cleitus, you'll soon learn that it doesn't matter if you bring back a hundred souls every night, you'll always have to go back out over and over again. Maybe you'll survive your first few decades. And for what? To see the Rookery grow rich off all your work? And if you make a mistake, then that's it—your life's forfeit," Andrés said, spittle flying from his mouths. "If you're lucky, you'll get to live in the city one day, but that's it. There's no higher station in life for you, not unless your family's royalty."

Andrés caught Cleitus's eyes scanning the wound on his right claw.

"Brother, you've come home without a soul." His pupils expanded into large disks. "My Gods, you have to face the—"

BWWWAAAAM!

The Rookery bellowed its second morning alarm.

Andrés turned his back on Cleitus and faced the Rookery. "You should go."

Cleitus scooped up his bags and unfurled his wings. The young Strider squatted and rocketed upward. Soon it hovered around one of the hundreds of platformed entrances encircling the bulge around the Rookery's midsection. Andrés saw Cleitus disappear into a darkened arch. Doubtless, the fledgling was heading down toward the Rookery's energy chambers to drop off his haul.

Andrés wondered if his friend Ramos was working the chambers this early. He gazed up at the blazing, pear-shaped sun—there was still time to find out!

CHAPTER 10
RACING THE CLOCK

Andrés sprinted forward, launching himself off the plateau and into the air. His leathery, veined wings splayed out and propelled him toward the Rookery.

He landed with a squelch on a wet platformed entrance. A thick, brown sludge dripped from his splayed foot. The Termitoidae were at work patching cracks on the Rookery's surface with klomm—a gag-inducing mixture of termite spit, shit, mud, and straw.

Andrés eyed dozens of the pale, bulbous-headed creatures clinging to the curved surface. The termites worked in teams of three: one stirred the viscous klomm with its slender front legs, while another used oversized mandibles to spread the batter for the third termite who stamped it all flat with a glistening, segmented bottom.

"Disgusting," Andrés hissed. Like most Striders, he harbored an intense hatred for the Crawlers, Phantids that walked on six or eight legs.

He looked down and admired his four slender, telescopic legs. The idea of extra appendages sprouting out from his abdomen sickened him. Someone within the entrance at his back retched. Vomit pattered in the darkness.

Andrés turned toward the sound. A Termitoidae crawled out from the arch, klomm dribbling from its glistening mandibles. Its translucent head angled back and forth as its antennae sniffed the air. It sensed Andrés but couldn't see him.

"Eyeless bastard." Andrés charged forward. He swiped the worker with his front claws, launching the termite off the Rookery's surface. It's spiny, translucent legs paddled the air as it fell to its death.

A lavender-tinged Strider, a construction supervisor, emerged from the archway. "Hey! Why did you do that? You think it's easy to train these beasts?" The supervisor's antennae bristled. "You're putting me behind—"

Andrés pinned the supervisor against the wall. "Workers like you don't get to raise your voice at hunters."

"So sorry, sir," he said. The black pupils in his faceted compound eyes quivered, breaking into smaller globules. "I'm just worried about my schedule."

Andrés inched his head closer. "They're just slaves, you fool. A hundred more are being born right now. Go get yourself a new one."

"Yes, you're right. I'm sorry."

Andrés stepped back and let the blue Strider go. He scuttled past and clambered off the platform.

Andrés turned and stepped through the entrance; a cold chill enveloped his exoskeleton. Built by termites, the Rookery was a perfectly insulated structure keeping the inside cool no matter how high the temperature outside rose.

For a moment, all Andrés could see was black, but his eyes adjusted and slowly focused on the rough, klomm-coated walls. The texture reminded him of stucco used to build human homes.

Andrés's thoughts turned back toward that boy and the decapitated ghost. Soon, the third alarm would cry out. He hoped that news of a Seer in the living world would blunt whatever punishment awaited him, but he still had some precious time left to him, and he'd use it to see his only friend in this world, Ramos.

Andrés sped through the empty tunnel and slowed down. The sunlight dimmed and he stood enveloped in shadow again.

Andrés growled and smacked the top of the tunnel with his claws over and over again. "Lazy buggers! Come on, I want to see my friend before I end up as the Marquis's lunch."

The vibrations stirred the enormous bioluminescent beetles that lived nestled in ditches on the tunnel's sides. There was just enough light to see their pill-shaped outlines.

There were very few human inventions that Andrés longed for, but electricity was one of them. Relying on Crawlers like beetles seemed backward to Andrés, but he had to make do with the biotechnology they had. He stamped his feet again, finally awakening the creatures.

He stepped back as thousands of wing casings opened and closed. The susurrations reminded Andrés of swords being drawn from leather sheaths. After a moment, the noise stopped. Slowly, the beetles ignited their segmented abdomens, casting an indigo glow against the walls. His path illuminated, Andrés charged through the tunnel and snatched a beetle from the ground, biting its head off and tossing the corpse behind him in one swift motion.

As he chewed, he wondered if he'd suffer the same fate at the hands of the Marquis. The thought turned his stomach; he spit out the half-eaten meal and marched onward.

CHAPTER 11
COOKING SOULS

The path dropped abruptly, and Andrés found himself plummeting down a wide shaft like a missile. Below, a circle of light shimmered like water. As Andrés exited through the opening, his wings fluttered open, keeping him hovering high above the Royal Energy Chamber—a single floor the width and breadth of the Rookery dedicated to the manufacturing of Qurdum, his people's only source of food.

Below, thousands of wide-mouthed terracotta pots, resting on furrows of black sand, were arranged within massive square plots. The arrangement gave the impression of an industrious, sprawling farm.

Striders buzzed out from the openings in the ceiling carrying dark orbs. They flew down toward the pots and handed over their prizes to pale, twig-like mantises, the Rookery's revered cooks. These specialized Striders made sure the captured souls stayed put and worked the wooden levers staked by each vessel.

Dust and flecks of klomm fell from the ceiling as the

Rookery's third alarm rocked the chamber. Andrés groaned. He was running out of time. His bulbous eyes frantically scanned the field below. Ramos was the only cook with a dark exoskeleton. He looked like a creeping shadow compared to his translucent colleagues, but there was no sign of his friend.

The best Andrés could do now was descend onto the plot Ramos worked and wait a few minutes before leaving to face the Marquis. Andrés crawled among the rows and admired the vessels, each one nearly six feet tall. All, except one, was topped with a thick, earthenware lid. Andrés peered into the open pot, his mandibles clicked together with excitement.

A dozen captured souls whirled around the smooth, copper-coated interior, orbiting an iron rod at the vessel's center. One after another, the orbs latched onto the metal shaft with a clink. A shadow crept over Andrés.

"You're in my way," a voice said.

Andrés turned and looked up. Looming over him was a thin mantis with rough scales the shape of leaves covering his mottled brown exoskeleton.

"Hello, Ramos. You're looking plump as ever."

Ramos's mandibles split open and his human face smiled. "Step aside, fledgling."

Andrés laughed. It was good to see a familiar face.

Friends were a rarity among Striders and one of the few relationships that developed without disdain were the ones between hunters and energy chamber cooks.

"You know, I'm svelte because I was born this way. My ancestors hunted from birch trees." Ramos picked up the large lid leaning against the pot with his claws and set it in place. He scratched the ground with his front, right foot, revealing the flared lip of a thick tube. "Here, use your tarsus to help me with the solution."

Andrés lowered his clawed forelimbs toward the buried duct. Thin slits opened from the tips of each claw. Slender two-pronged appendages wriggled out from the gashes. The pink flesh on their rounded tips peeled back, revealing two sets of human forefingers and thumbs.

Andrés pinched the edges of the tube with his squirming digits and pulled his arms back. The duct slithered out from the earth, raising a small cloud of dust. He held the translucent piping over his head and turned toward his friend. "Is this long enough?"

Ramos nodded. "Perfect. I'll take it from here."

Andrés stepped back as the cook attached the tubing to the lid. Ramos pushed a wooden lever forward and the ground gurgled as acid pumped up through the tube and into the pot.

Steam sizzled from the edges of the lid as the vinegar smelling slop reacted with the copper. The souls inside screeched as the liquid stretched, pulled, and reshaped the building blocks of their consciousnesses.

The screams were comforting, helping Andrés forget about the Seer and the Marquis. This is why he wanted to watch his friend cook.

Ramos pulled back on the lever to empty the chamber and pulled open the lid. As the steam evaporated, Andrés plucked the end product from the violent process—a single Qurdum, a glowing brick that resembled a fetus and could feed a Phantid brood for a week.

"This is what it's all about, isn't it?" Andrés asked, cradling the luminous stone.

Ramos cocked his head to the side. "Are you ok?"

There was no point in burdening Ramos with the knowledge that he might never return. Instead, he handed over the Qurdum.

"I need to get going." Andrés turned his head upward and eyed one of the exit holes at the center of the roof. As his wing casings opened, Andrés gazed at his friend. "You're the best cook here, you know that?"

Ramos bowed. "Thank you for saying so, my friend."

Andrés smiled and rocketed upward just as the fourth alarm blared.

CHAPTER 12
THE MARQUIS

Andrés didn't care that he was late now.

Instead, he imagined the Marquis gagging to death on a wad of klomm. Dozens of bloody scenarios rolled through his mind as he flew through the zigzagging tunnels.

A light at the end of the path nearly blinded Andrés as he fluttered into the hollow center of the Rookery. He hovered in place, giving his compound eyes time to adjust to the glow.

He marveled at the adobe-colored Royal Palace. Ringed by a series of concentric battlements, the massive castle floated on a bed of gigantic, downturned amethyst crystals that rotated in the darkness like a gaudy chandelier.

At the palace's center bulged a faceted glass dome modeled off the Marquis's eye, but on a gargantuan scale. A black pupil, the size of a small pond, bubbled from beneath the dome's shimmering emerald surface and tracked Andrés as he circled the palace.

You're late! the Marquis's voice growled inside Andrés's mind. *I expected you inside my throne room five minutes ago!*

"My apologies, Lord," Andrés said, landing at the entrance. He faced two enormous arched doors. Their surfaces were decorated with glazed brick reliefs of Striders battling scorpions, beetles, and other Phantids.

Don't you dare come in through there! Use the Crawler entrance.

Andrés hissed as a small hole puckered open near the side of the right door. Smudged streaks of black feces coated the interior of the new opening left behind by his six-legged cousins. Andrés flattened himself and crawled through like a common cockroach, gagging all the way, and popped out into the antechamber.

Two female Striders stood guard in front of the throne room's golden doors, baring their human smiles at him. Andrés assumed that they were sizing him up to see what wee bits would be left over for them once the Marquis was done with him. The warrior on the right licked her lips as she stepped aside. The doors opened inward and Andrés stepped through.

A column of black smoke churned at the center of the glittering, high-ceilinged chamber. The towering funnel picked up speed and stopped suddenly. Andrés ducked as flecks of darkness spiraled outward like blurred arrowheads. What vapors remained, thinned around the imposing outline of the Marquis who bobbed left and right. Like all Striders, the Marquis used the swaying motion to better gauge the distance between himself and potential prey.

One microsecond, Andrés thought, bowing and calculating the time it would take for his Lord's raptorial claws to reach his head. When the death blow didn't arrive, he looked up at his master who had crawled back to sit in his throne, a mass of pale, purple orchid petals the size of barn doors.

Andrés struggled to focus on the Marquis. His body was the color of alabaster, streaked with pink veins that followed the contours of his thick exoskeleton; the camouflage blended perfectly against the pale petals around him. From his bishop miter-shaped head, bright-red, feathered antennae extended from the base and fluttered like candle flames as he spoke.

"This is your first failure in over two centuries," the Marquis growled, capturing one of the many Qurdums floating around his throne. He tossed the brick into his segmented mouth and swallowed it whole. "Rumors are swirling, Andrés. Rumors of a Seer. Is this true or did you just fuck up?"

"Marquis, great Lord and protector," Andrés said, kneeling. He raised his head and exposed his thin neck, the ultimate sign of submission. "I come to you seeking forgiveness for my failure and ask for leniency, considering the situation."

The pupils in the Marquis's round eyes exploded into pulsing stars. "Stop stalling! Is there a Seer? Yes, or no?"

The mouth beneath Andrés's mandibles grinned. He now knew with certainty that he'd be spared. "Yes, my Lord. A living boy can see me," he said, risking a direct gaze with the Marquis, adding, "And he touched me."

The Marquis exhaled a dark, spiked bubble and sucked it back in. "This is impossible! The living are cut off. Have been cut off. There hasn't been a Seer in their world since the traitor Ugallu gifted the Mesopotamians the Knowledge."

Andrés stumbled backward as the Marquis rushed forward with an outstretched claw.

"Please, my Lord. Please look at my memories."

The Marquis stepped back and nodded his head. Andrés composed himself. Sharing memories was painful, but never fatal. And in this case, it would stop the beating. He turned his head down and drew in a long, deep breath.

Using the sharp spike at the tip of his right claw, Andrés plunged the weapon he was born with into the center of his head. He carved a line toward his mandibles and pulled away. Rivulets of pale green dripped from the wound and into his jaws. He tasted of salted caramel.

"My Lord?" Andrés said, shaking.

The Marquis leaned in, steadied his subject's head with the sides of his forelimbs, and sucked the globules from Andrés's armored face. Memories flooded into the Marquis's mind, and he saw the moment Edgar Tooms latched onto Andrés's claw.

"You weren't exaggerating, Andrés," the Marquis said, backing away. "This boy is powerful and dangerous."

"I think so too." Andrés wiped the Marquis's cinnamon-scented spit off his face. He hoped his revulsion stayed hidden beneath his downturned gaze as the smell stung his pores. "What should we do, my Lord?"

"What you're going to do is find a way to kill this boy. Discreetly, of course. And to do that, you'll need an expert's help."

Andrés knew the name before his Lord even spoke it: Malva, the Ghost Scythe; the Marquis's insane niece. Phantids like Andrés had limited abilities to interact with the physical world, but Malva had talents that could influence the planes above like no other Strider could.

Andrés shuddered. The Ghost Scythe also had a reputation of hunting her own kind for sport; and being a relation of the Marquis meant she'd never suffer the consequences.

"She'll have strict orders not to harm you, Andrés," the Marquis said, reading his mind. He cocked his head to the side and twitched his antennae. "There. I've already sent word to Malva about our situation. Luther here will see you out."

Out from a hole in the far corner of the throne room marched the Marquis's personal secretary, a shimmering blue scorpion. Andrés leaped backward and stared down at the creature's twelve beady eyes, hairy legs, and oily carapace. Pinched in one of its muscular claws was a Qurdum.

"Cousin, this is for you," Luther said, waving the prize at Andrés. "You'll need your strength for the task ahead."

Andrés snarled. Rookery decorum forced him to bow and thank any Phantid who offered a Qurdum. There was no escaping the humiliation that was about to unfold—obviously orchestrated by his master. Andrés lowered himself and muttered, "Thank you."

The Marquis laughed and waved for the two Phantids to leave. The throne room doors opened, and Andrés and Luther walked backward toward the exit.

CHAPTER 13
MALVA THE GHOST SCYTHE

"Malva wants to meet you in the dining hall," Luther said, sprinting ahead through the hallway.

Of course she wants to meet there. She probably wants my head on a platter, Andrés thought, shaking his head.

"Cousin, did you hear me?" the scorpion asked, stopping mid-stride.

"Yes, I did. And I don't need a chaperone, Luther," Andrés hissed. He resented having to speak to the scorpion as if he was an equal. If Luther wasn't part of the Marquis's royal court, he'd have gutted the eight-legged beast by now. Luckily, the little secretary wasn't known for long conversations.

"Very well," Luther said, tapping his hard belly on the floor as a sign of respect.

"Fucking Crawler," Andrés mumbled, turning toward the end of the hallway.

He sped through the hallway and entered the palace's sacred center. Marble stairs and gilded bridges spanned the interior like Baroque cobwebs and hundreds of other

Striders like him went about their business trailing black clouds behind them as they walked and talked. The puffs covered the palace's domed roof in layers of waxy soot.

Andrés took the quickest route and entered the unguarded dining hall. The Ghost Scythe sat at the end of a long wooden slab. Malva was twice the size of Andrés, and her bone-white segmented body was streaked with shimmering purple that pulsed with her heartbeat. Layers of thin plates the shape of flower petals flowed along the ridges of her arms and legs.

"Malva, it's a pleasure to meet you," Andrés said, walking toward her.

She bobbed to the side just like her uncle did moments ago, and as Andrés reached striking distance, the organic machinery of her jaw parted, revealing smooth human skin and an impish nose. A single, deeply carved laugh line ran from the corner of her left nostril toward the edge of her pale, pink lips.

Andrés's cock hardened into a quivering green dagger that pressed painfully against the interior of his lower abdomen. Invisible wisps of pheromones wafted from his shell. Malva sneered as her fluttering antennae picked up the sticky, cinnamon scent. It was impossible for males of his species to hide their excitement. The best Andrés could do was limit the concentration of desire released into the air by clenching his pores tighter.

"Uncle says we have a job to do, eh?"

As she spoke, bubbles of black clouds appeared in front of her head as if stippled onto the air by an unseen brush and quickly evaporated.

Andrés lowered his head and nodded.

"Don't be shy, Andrés," Malva said. She whipped her

thin antenna backward and smiled. "You and I are going to have a blast in the world above. I adore little boys."

Malva's husky voice and unique breath unnerved Andrés even more than the Marquis's presence had. Perhaps it was a familial talent. He shook the thought out of his head and locked eyes on his new partner.

"I'm ready when you are."

"Very well," Malva said. "Let's go on a little reconnaissance mission, shall we?"

CHAPTER 14

SPIES LIKE US

The trip to Eperu, the world of the living, took minutes compared to the desert trek Andrés normally endured to reach the porous border between his world and Edgar's.

As royalty, Malva had a personal teleportation chamber installed in her office. From there, the two Striders used a clay tablet carved with the coordinates of the Tooms' family home and marched through a darkened, arched doorway toward their destination.

Malva landed first and scuttled toward a thick group of bushes in the backyard. She beckoned Andrés over as he appeared from a dark cloud, confused by the unfamiliar nighttime surroundings.

"Why are we outside?" he asked, finding a concealed position not too close to his new partner.

"Why are Strider males so nervous?" Malva snapped. Her pale white exoskeleton blushed a deep red as if gallons of blood suddenly flowed under her armor.

Andrés took a step backward. "I'm not nervous. I just don't understand why we're out here instead—"

"I want to take some time to get a feel for the boy's territory," Malva snarled. "And I want to see it without being seen right away."

A light in the attic turned their attention upward.

"There!" Andrés said, pointing toward the floating outline of Charles Tooms's head. "Why don't I just fly up now before the boy can do anything about it?"

"Patience, Andrés. These decapitated ones are rare and make for tasty Qurdum," Malva said, rubbing her claws together and flashing lavender eyes at Andrés. "Did you carve the sigil inside their home correctly?"

"Of course. I've been doing this for two hundred years," Andrés snapped, his pupils flattening into thin dashes. "We can get in and out of the house whenever we want."

"Good. Then let's get some eyes and ears inside the house."

Malva let out a low whistle and twitched her antennae. In response, thousands of unseen insects chittered and clicked. The grass around the two Striders flattened as a gleaming carpet of cockroaches clumped around Malva's legs.

"Disgusting!" Andrés said, creeping backward. The insects in this world disturbed him and always turned his stomach.

"Now, now, Andrés. These are our friends," Malva said, lowering her head closer to the ground for the mass to hear her simple orders: "You lot get in there and report back everything that you see and hear."

The roaches sped toward the Tooms' home and disappeared within its cracks and shadows. At that very moment, a twig snapped behind Andrés and Malva. They turned as a young girl zipped around them and through the backyard, crushing a few of the slower roaches with her bicycle's thick, rubber wheels.

56   LUIS PAREDES

turned as a young girl zipped around them and through the backyard, crushing a few of the slower roaches with her bicycle's thick, rubber wheels.

CHAPTER 15
CLARA RUSHES TO EDGAR

Edgar's voicemail didn't make much sense, but the panicked warble in his voice convinced Clara that it was an emergency, so she dropped her paint brushes and rushed out the door, lamenting that she had missed the call hours ago.

He was a five-minute bicycle ride away and her mind mulled over the possibilities a trip to Edgar's house would bring through every second of the trip. Maybe Edgar's mom hit him again? Clara shook her head. As neglectful as her parents were, she didn't envy the mercurial mother Edgar lived with.

At an intersection, a darker thought entered Clara's mind: Opa Chuck might be hurt. The first time the old man deflated, she held Edgar as he cried over the spot where his grandfather's head supposedly lay flat. An hour later, she leaped for joy when Edgar said Opa was up and floating.

Or maybe this really was about bugs. He said something about a giant insect in the house. Clara grinned at the thought. She kept butterfly and beetle specimens pinned to her bedroom wall and had just enough space for something as large as an Eastern Giant Swallowtail or a Hercules beetle. She peddled faster, eager to find out what species of creepy-crawly had Edgar so scared.

Clara eyed a shortcut: a neighbor's side entrance that ran through Edgar's backyard. She pumped the peddles and leaned forward. The passageway's brick surface rattled the chunky, rainbow-colored bracelets on her wrists as the bike picked up speed.

Clara jumped over a coiled garden hose and popped onto the smooth grass in Edgar's yard. She swerved around what looked like two enormous leaf mounds next to a bush and nearly lost control as the bike's tires wobbled over a slick patch of earth.

That was close, Clara thought. Edgar's mom always complained about her paint-streaked and marker-smudged clothing. She'd never let her in if she was covered in mud.

She glanced back at the mounds.

For a moment she thought she saw the leaf piles shuffle forward.

CHAPTER 16
SHARING VISIONS

"It's nine at night, Clara," Margaret groaned, leaning against the door frame. She flicked a half-smoked cigarette over Clara's head. It sizzled in an unseen puddle. "Some of us adults have to be at work before the sun rises."

"Um, hi Mrs. Tooms. Right. I'm sorry, but Edgar wanted me to come over. I would have come earlier, but I was painting. An oil painting. And, well, I missed his call, and by the time I heard his voicemail it was almost nine," Clara said, listing off the conditions that led her to the door so late.

"Aren't you cold in that?" Margaret asked, giving Clara's blue, paint-spattered tank top a disdaining look.

Clara pulled at the shirt's fabric with her fingertips and let it snap back. The motion jangled the pentacles, crosses, stars, ankhs, and other charms dangling from thin, gold chains on her neck.

"Nah. It's a pretty warm night." Clara paused and wiped her nose with her fist. "Um, can I come in now?"

Margaret rolled her eyes and opened the door. Edgar

thundered down the stairs and stood at the landing. His bloodshot eyes had a glossy, crazed look. They almost distracted Clara from Edgar's frizzled hair, chapped lips, and pale, clammy skin. She'd never seen her best friend look so . . . crazy.

"He's been a mess all day long. Going on about giant bugs." Margaret raised a palm above her head. "I've had it up to here with him today. Just look at the state of him."

Edgar's head drooped. He patted down his hair with a few palm strokes and glanced up at Clara. "Thanks for coming."

"Yeah, of course. Your crazy message said it was important," she said, punching his shoulder and laughing. A smile erupted across Edgar's face.

"Yeah! There's my Edgar!" Clara paused. Why in the world did she say, my Edgar? "I mean, you look better smiling. That's all."

Margaret raised an eyebrow and stumbled back to the living room. "Ok, have fun, you two. No funny business."

"Moooom!" Edgar groaned. "We're just going up to my room to draw for a bit. I need Clara for an art—"

Before Edgar could finish his sentence, Clara rushed up the stairs. Edgar's feet thumped close behind. She was eager to leave behind her moment of awkwardness and beat Edgar at another foot race.

She reached the second-floor landing and quickened her pace, clambering over the attic stairs and bounding into Edgar's room, arms raised, like a victorious marathon runner.

Clara grinned as Edgar limped through the threshold.

"You know, you just scared Opa Chuck half to death running in here like that," Edgar said, hands on his knees.

"Opa's already a ghost, silly," Clara said.

"Still, let's not do that again," Edgar said, making his way to the bed. He sat and groaned.

Clara smiled and dropped into a cross-legged position in front of Edgar. "Soooo, tell me. What happened, Edgar?" She scooched closer, eager to hear what was on his mind.

Edgar exhaled and rubbed his eyes with his fists. For a moment, Clara thought he would start shivering, but instead he started to narrate, without taking his eyes off the floor, what grandfather and grandson had experienced: the strange carving, the ghoulish blue light, the giant mantis and its horrid face, and the short fight Edgar had with the creature.

Then he stopped talking and just stared at her. She didn't know what to say, but she could tell by Edgar's raised eyebrows that he was waiting for her to say something, anything.

"This is all so . . . weird, Edgar," she managed.

Edgar's eyes widened. "Weird? Yeah, it's really fucking weird. What do you think I should do?"

Clara stood up. He'd never snapped at her before. Something had him spooked, but could he have really seen gigantic mantises? She pursed her lips. Were giant bugs any stranger than believing in Opa Chuck?

Edgar winced as if an invisible hand smacked his cheek. His eyes focused on a spot just a few feet above his head. Clara had seen that look and interaction before—he was talking to his grandfather. After a moment, he nodded, stared at his hands, and exhaled.

"What's wrong?" Clara asked.

"Opa says that I shouldn't talk to you like that." Edgar

stood and walked toward the attic window at the far end of his room. He gazed at the backyard and shook his head. "I'm so sorry, Clara. I didn't mean to snap at you."

She followed and stood next to Edgar. "It's ok. Listen, I have no idea what to do, but my Aunt Ginnie says burning sage or rosemary is a good way to cleanse bad spirits from a house."

"You think she has anything better than herbs?"

"I'm sorry, Edgar. I wish I knew what we could do, but I don't have much experience in this sort of—"

Edgar recoiled from the window. "Oh, God!"

"What? Is it back?"

"No. It's a roach on the window. A big one."

"Let me see! I love bugs," Clara said, pressing next to Edgar as roaches with glossy wings settled on the glass. They landed with tiny thumps and arranged themselves like living jigsaw pieces until the view outside was obscured by a swarm of writhing bellies and wriggling legs.

"Well, that's gross," Clara said, tapping the glass. When that didn't startle them, she slapped her palm on the window. The bugs fluttered off.

Edgar clasped his head with both hands. "Look! It's back, and it brought a friend."

Clara gazed outside. She couldn't see anything besides the illuminated yard, the mounds of leaves she narrowly avoided earlier, and the nearby shrubbery. "Really? Where?"

Edgar jabbed his finger at the source. Clara squinted and pressed her forehead against the window, but she couldn't see anything out of the ordinary. She cupped her hands over her eyes and leaned forward. Still nothing.

"I'm sorry that I can't see what you see," Clara said, resting her head on Edgar's shoulder. He sighed. Clara's heart raced. This was the first time she had snuggled so close to him, and it felt . . . right.

Without thinking, she grasped Edgar's hand. An electric shock slithered through her fingers, up her arm, and into her head. Her eyesight blurred and refocused with razor-sharp clarity. What she thought of as leaf piles, solidified into two enormous insects squatting on the grass. Their thin legs bowed out like spiders. Clara screamed.

"I'm so sorry, Clara. Is it because I squeezed too hard? I didn't mean to," Edgar stammered, hiding his hands behind his back.

Clara shook her head and pointed toward the yard below, but the creatures were gone, replaced by the dark mounds.

"I saw them," she whispered. "When we held hands, I saw them! One's a big green one and the other looks like it's made out of giant flower petals, right?"

"Yeah! But how's that possible?"

"I don't know, but let's do it again," Clara insisted, rushing to the window. She eyed the plain looking bushes. "Ok, there's nothing there. Quick, give me your hand!"

Clara's vision blurred and then sharpened again, bringing to focus the strange beings spying on the house. Goosebumps rippled across her skin. The mantises were huge! She'd need giant stakes to pin them to her wall!

Clara knocked on the glass and shouted, "We can see you two!"

CHAPTER 17
RECOGNITION

The Striders locked eyes on the children above and cocked their heads to the side. Malva growled.

"What did she say?" Andrés asked.

"This is worse than Uncle thought. The girl can see us now too."

A delegation of cockroaches crawled back, and Malva lowered her claw, letting the insects swarm along her limb. The roaches skittered across the smooth outer shell or crawled between the rows of long white barbs studding the underside of Malva's claw. They pooled at her claw's hinge, a brown, chittering mass of fluttering wings and twitching antennae.

"I don't speak gibberish. What are they saying?" Andrés asked.

"They report what we just saw. The boy's a powerful Seer: he can transfer his abilities. We need to take care of them quickly, but not now," Malva said, shaking the roaches off her arm. "We'll plan our attack on the house. A simple pincer move should do it."

Andrés nodded and stepped backward to disappear in a cloud of ink Malva had spread behind their bodies.

CHAPTER 18
CLARA MEETS OPA CHUCK

Clara's feet ached. She'd been standing in front of the attic window with Edgar for most of the night, watching the yard to make sure the giant mantises were really gone.

The moon peeked out from slate gray clouds, casting a gossamer glow over the backyard; the light gave them a better view of the charred grass the two giant mantises left behind.

A plump raccoon waddled over and sniffed the darkened spot. Even from this distance, Clara could see the masked bandit's nose twitch and curdle at the same time. It dug at the boundary between healthy green shoots and wilted brown blades with its slender, black paws. Then it jumped backward as if shocked by something in the dirt.

"Did you see that? That's the third critter hurt by whatever those things left behind," Clara said, watching the raccoon scamper back into the shadows.

"At least it didn't choke to death like that skunk. Come on, it doesn't seem like those giant bugs are coming back,"

Edgar said, letting go of Clara's hand. "Let's go downstairs for a bit."

Clara flexed her fingers. She didn't realize that they'd been holding onto each other the entire time. *That was nice,* she thought and skipped after Edgar as he made his way toward the door. She stopped mid-stride and covered her mouth with both hands.

This isn't possible! Clara thought.

"What's wrong?" Edgar asked, turning.

"I can see him," she mumbled through stacked palms.

"Who?"

"Me. She can see me," Charles said, emerging nose-first, from the floorboards. He rose into the air and hovered just to the right of his grandson's shoulder. "Hello, Clara. It's nice to finally meet you."

"It's true! I knew it! I knew it was all true!" Clara shouted, running around the room. She leaped onto Edgar's bed and hopped on the mattress.

"This is amazing!" Edgar yelled, joining in on the rumpus.

"Opa Chuck! Opa Chuck! Opa Chuck!" they shouted.

"Get off the bed, ya wonkadoodles, or you'll both fall off," Charles said, speeding toward the two, laughing.

Clara shrieked as Charles zipped over. As nice as it was to see Edgar's grandfather, the sight of a pale, decapitated head rushing through the air was jarring and she instinctively slapped Charles's nose when he zoomed too close.

He spun backward and disappeared into the nearby wall. Clara turned toward Edgar, her eyes wide, expecting a flurry of curses.

Edgar's face tensed and then slackened.

Clara exhaled in relief as he dropped to his knees and

laughed, and before she knew it, she was laughing with him.

"Well, I'm glad you two are finding this funny," Charles said, reemerging from the plaster.

"I'm so sorry! I didn't mean to do that," Clara said.

"It's ok. But how in the world is this possible?" Charles asked, drifting close to his grandson's shoulder again. "Only Edgar's been able to get a hold of me."

"Yeah, this is really weird," Edgar said, wiping away the tears of laughter from his ruddy cheeks. He looked down at his hands. "I think it's the Catch, Opa."

"What's the Catch?" Clara asked.

"It's what I call my power, um, my ability to hold Opa," Edgar explained.

Clara raised an eyebrow.

"It's easier if I show you."

Edgar hopped off the bed and walked behind his grandfather. He held one outstretched palm above his grandfather's head and the other palm below what little remained of the old man's neck.

"I just concentrate on feeling for Opa's head and then—"

"Zap!" Charles shouted, grinning.

Clara flinched. They were joking, but she could hear a faint crackle in the air.

Charles's pale skin pulsed fire engine red. One moment he was floating and then the next, falling as if dragged by an unseen anchor. Clara yelled a warning, but Charles slipped out of Edgar's grip and bounced several times on the floor before landing face up a few inches from her feet.

"A little help, please," Charles said, staring up at Clara.

She bent down and scooped the head up between her

hands. She scrunched her eyes and held back a nervous laugh. "You feel . . . weird."

Charles rolled his eyes. "So I've been told. Well, at least you didn't throw up in my face like Edgar over there."

"Hey! That was just the first time. I was a little kid back then."

Clara laughed and handed Charles to Edgar.

"You just did it, Clara," Edgar said, shifting Charles to his favorite position—cradled in the crook of his right arm. "You didn't even have to think about it."

"She's a keeper, Edgar," Charles said.

Clara stood, beaming.

"Opa!" Edgar groaned.

Clara smiled at her best friend, who coughed nervously and avoided her gaze.

"Well, what do we do now?" Edgar asked.

Clara mulled the question over. At some point, they would need to ask for help from the adults in their lives. If they tried explaining everything, they'd never believe their stories. They'd need proof of some kind. It was too late to take photos of the giant bugs, but Clara remembered she kept a few sketchpads and colored pencils squirreled away in Edgar's closet for when inspiration struck.

"We need to document everything we've experienced. This is like, a brand-new discovery. People need to know what's out there," she said, rummaging through Edgar's belongings.

"Wait, how are we going to do that?" Edgar asked.

"With these!" Clara said, brandishing art supplies in both hands.

CHAPTER 19

MORNING SKETCHES

Charles woke to the sound of scratching. He puttered upward and tried to suss out the source of the noise, but his exhausted eyes refused to focus, no matter how hard he blinked.

The scraping grew louder and faster.

Edgar groaned and pulled the sheets over his head. "Stop making that noise, Opa. It sounds like the symbols are carving themselves into the wall again."

Charles's eyes widened and focused at last. For a moment he was convinced that Andrés was back, but a glance at the bedroom floor quickly set his mind at ease—Clara was still drawing.

They had spent the night detailing the creatures they saw while Clara sketched them out in vivid detail. Edgar rolled out of bed and walked toward the pile of drawings that had grown since he fell asleep. Charles noticed a small, square sheet of paper stuck to his foot—it was Edgar's drawing of the symbol that appeared and disappeared from the living room wall.

"You didn't show me that one," Clara said, snatching the paper from Edgar's bare heel. She turned the sketch around and paused. "That's cuneiform."

"Cunei-what?" Edgar asked.

"Cuneiform. An old alphabet people used hundreds and hundreds of years ago. I have no idea what this means," Clara answered, tapping the page. "But my aunt Ginnie knows all about it. She's a professor at NYU. Cuneiform's her thing."

"Do you think she could tell us what it means?" Charles asked.

Clara smiled. She snapped a photo of the symbol with her phone and texted it to her aunt. The phone buzzed back with Ginnie's simple command: *Come over now!*

CHAPTER 20
AUNT GINNIE

Edgar peddled hard and leaned into his bicycle's handlebars as he rumbled downhill. Clara followed closely on her own bike.

"You still with us, Opa?" Edgar shouted.

"Twelve o'clock high and doing fine," Charles shouted as he zoomed through the air a few feet above the children. "Watch this, you two."

Charles rocketed up and performed a few loop-de-loops in the air before rejoining Edgar and Clara on their way into town.

"That was awesome!" Clara shouted over the sound of the playing card flapping against her bike's spokes.

Edgar smiled. Just a day ago the thought of Opa Chuck leaving the house seemed impossible. For years, the furthest his grandfather could get was a few feet into the backyard or front yard. Any further, and he risked a blinding headache and a rapid loss of whatever filled his head, leaving him flopping on the floor like a pale, see-through flounder.

But today, once they were two blocks away from the house, they knew deflation wasn't an issue anymore. Things had changed. Edgar's stomach gurgled and his heart skipped a beat. He didn't know if those changes were for the better or worse. He had to believe this change was for the best.

"Kiddo, you look worried," Charles said.

He was never good at masking his feelings. Even on his best acting days, Opa could pick up on the nuances of anxiety that crawled over Edgar's face.

"Nah, it's nothing, Opa. I'm just so glad we walked you out of the house! There was no way we were going to leave you behind, not with those things around," Edgar said, swerving around an old woman pushing a cart down the sidewalk.

It was tempting though, he thought. Aunt Ginnie's text promised answers to the nightmare they were facing and even Opa suggested they peddle along without him.

"Yeah! We're a team, Opa. I told you this would work!" Clara said, popping a wheelie.

"Show-off!" Edgar rolled his eyes and huffed. It was, in fact, Clara's idea that they test the limits of his grandfather's invisible tether. And, as usual, she was right.

Edgar glanced up. Opa smiled as the wind pushed back his wispy hair. Strange, Edgar thought, the wind had never touched his grandfather before. Opa looked down and caught Edgar staring.

"You worry too much, Edgar. Whatever fills me up seems to be holding. Our abilities seem to be improving," Charles said, flying between the children. "How much further, Clara?"

"Let's stop ahead," she said, turning onto the town's main drag and skidding to a stop.

Clara and Edgar locked their bikes in front of a hot dog shop and walked down an alley between an Italian café and an ice cream parlor. The cement path that snaked behind the shops gave way to clay bricks covered in gnarled roots that led up to a secluded patch of trees on a hill.

"Come on," Clara said, padding up the faded bricks. "My aunt will know what to do."

The sun-bleached orange and red steps led to a dilapidated, three-story Dutch colonial that Edgar was sure had seen better days. Moldy gutters hung off the gabled roof; the faded cheddar-yellow paint peeled away in strips, revealing the dimpled gray stucco underneath; and many of the windows were boarded up.

Opa whistled and jutted his chin toward the wreck of the house. "She lives in there?"

"I thought she was some kind of professor in the city," Edgar said. "Doesn't she make a ton of money?"

"Aunt Ginnie loves two things, you guys, books and teaching. Nothing else gets much attention. I know it looks bad, but my aunt knows her stuff."

The door creaked open and Clara's aunt stood at the threshold, her head almost touching the lintel. A gust of morning wind caught the fabric of her cherry-red silk kaftan, billowing it around her pear-shaped frame like a sail. Thick copper bracelets jangled as she stretched her arms out, and Clara skipped into her aunt's embrace like a moth to a flame.

"My little muffin! It's great to see you, and so good of you to send me that drawing!" Aunt Ginnie beamed, hugging her niece. She turned to Edgar and brushed back a wisp of auburn hair behind her ear. "And who's this delectable little gentleman?"

Clara rolled her eyes. "Tía! Stop being so weird. This is Edgar. He drew the symbol I sent you. It appeared in his house yesterday."

"Hello, ma'am."

"Don't be shy, Edgar. You've seen something very special, and you've come to the right place. Only a handful of people know what that symbol means," she said, tousling Edgar's hair.

"Really?"

"Yes, really. Please, come in. I'll get us some drinks and you can tell me everything about what you saw—and don't leave out any details!" she said, walking into the house.

Edgar hesitated. He glanced at Opa, hovering by his side. His grandfather frowned and bobbed up and down—his version of a shrug.

Clara's aunt was intimidating, and the darkened interior of the house did little to calm his nerves. Edgar's reluctance was greeted by a firm shove from Clara that sent him tumbling through the entrance.

CHAPTER 21

PHANTID HISTORY

The smell of moldy paper, dust, and wood wafted into Edgar's nostrils as his eyes adjusted to the ill-lit front room. He soon marveled at the stacks of paper and books blocking the stairs that led up to the second floor.

"Welcome to Casa Diaz!" Clara shouted, making her way through the parlor.

Hands stuffed in pockets, Edgar followed, and then stopped. Every square inch of the home's cracked, plaster walls were covered with Clara's artwork and picture frames—pictures of Aunt Ginnie on her travels through the Middle East.

The images reminded Edgar of the snapshots his father had sent home when he was in Iraq. Aunt Ginnie's smile in the photos reminded him of his father's smile.

There was something else about the photos and the people in them that held his attention. One face appeared next to Aunt Ginnie's more than any of the others: a bald, elderly man with an impressive handlebar mustache and wedged beard. He seemed to never be without the thin-rimmed sunglasses that he wore, even at night.

"That's Sol Balam, professor of Egyptology and Assyri-ology at Brown University. He's a good friend," Aunt Ginnie said, winking and nudging Edgar in the ribs with her elbow. "Head into the living room. I want to show you something."

Edgar walked through the dining area as Aunt Ginnie ducked into the kitchen. Even more piles of books covered the table and chairs along with half-filled coffee mugs, granola bar wrappers, half-eaten sandwiches, moldy banana peels, and crumpled papers.

Charles floated over the debris and shook his head. "What a mess."

"Yeah, and Mom thinks my room's bad," Edgar said.

He heard the clink of glasses and the faucet rattle to life.

"What was that, Edgar?" Aunt Ginnie asked from the kitchen.

"Nothing, just admiring all your . . . books," Edgar said.

"Be nice," Clara said, skipping her way into the living room. She plopped onto a plush blue couch and beckoned Edgar to join her, but his eyes were locked on the book-shelves that surrounded the space and the hundreds, maybe thousands, of books packed into the shelves like mushroom gills. Charles puttered toward Clara while Aunt Ginnie made her way into the living room with a tray of drinks.

Edgar's eyes drifted to an antique rolltop desk sitting in the corner. Propped up on the desk's dusty upper deck, stood three clay cylinders, their surfaces deeply etched with triangles and dashes around the canisters.

"Those scratches . . ." Edgar muttered, half to himself, as he walked toward the desk. He rubbed one of the cylinders with a finger. "That's cuneiform, right?"

"Yes. Very good. If you like those, then you're going to love what's inside this," Aunt Ginnie said, tapping the cover of a book sitting on a small, teak coffee table.

Edgar stared wide-eyed at the circle flanked by triangles printed on the cover. The title read, *The Forgotten Gods of the Ancient Akkadian Empire.*

"That's the symbol!" Edgar shouted. He sat down on the blue couch between Aunt Ginnie and Clara. Charles bobbed just above Edgar's shoulder.

"The archaeologist who wrote this, Francis Saltus, discovered three clay tablets in Baghdad in the early 1900s," Aunt Ginnie said. "The cuneiform on each slab tells the story of a race of demons that hunted human beings and feasted on their souls."

Aunt Ginnie turned to the kids and stuck her tongue out in mock disgust. Edgar and Clara laughed.

"These beings terrorized the Akkadian people that lived along the banks of the Tigris River." Aunt Ginnie opened the book to a photograph of a relief carved onto stone. "This is the only known visual representation of the creatures."

The image showcased tall humanoids with many limbs, blank faces, and long beards holding people by their legs or necks. The monsters stood on undulating mounds of earth as three others floated in the sky.

"It's a beautiful tablet by the way. I held it once at the

Iraq Museum in Baghdad back in the seventies. I can still remember what the carvings felt like," Aunt Ginnie said. "The slab was smooth expect for the details—they are raised stone and full of texture. You could even feel the veins in the wings of the ones flying."

"What are they?" Edgar asked, picking up a glass of water from the table.

"Saltus called them Phantids, phantom insects. Apparently, there were different species of these creatures, but the ones in that carving are called Striders."

"What happened to them?" Clara asked.

"Around 750 BC they were banished from our world by Kaus-malaka, the king of Edom. He was gifted weapons to drive the demons away. Well, further away. The story says they were cast deep into the underworld."

"What if they can still come up? Into our world?" Edgar asked, taking another slow sip.

Aunt Ginnie raised an eyebrow and picked up the lone shot glass from the table and knocked back the amber fluid.

"It's just a story, Edgar. A myth. But here's the strange thing, no one in the academic community seems to know about this man's discovery. After 1918, there's no mention of Saltus, the ghost insects, or his work. As far as I know, only a handful of people, like me and Sol, know about these creatures."

Aunt Ginnie slammed the book shut.

"So, how did you come across that symbol, young man?"

Edgar looked at Clara.

"Tell her!" Clara said.

"Those markings appeared in my house yesterday," Edgar said, shifting uncomfortably on the couch.

Aunt Ginnie leaned back and smoothed the fabric of her kaftan and focused her eyes on Edgar. He was surprised to see such honest interest in her face. It was the same look Clara had when he trusted her with his secret.

CHAPTER 22

SHARING SECRETS

Confident he was in good company, Edgar told her everything—starting from the first time he saw Opa Chuck to the appearance of the giant mantis.

"And then it . . . it grabbed Opa!" he said, heaving in bucketfuls of air. Aunt Ginnie placed a hand on his back and rubbed until his breathing settled. Edgar hadn't realized how lucky it was that Opa Chuck survived.

Edgar dropped his head between his knees and gulped in a series of sharp breaths. He moaned and rocked back and forth on the couch with his hands wrapped around his head.

"Edgar's starting to hyperventilate." Charles nudged Clara's shoulder with his forehead. "You two have to calm him down before he passes out."

Clara nodded and placed a hand on Edgar's knee and squeezed.

"It's ok, Edgar. Just listen to my voice. You're going to be—"

"I can still hear the sound of its claw crackling under

my fingertips. It was . . . disgusting," he said, rubbing his palms together. Edgar stared at Aunt Ginnie. "He called me a little swine. I'm a good kid. It's not my fault that I can see things."

"You didn't do anything wrong, honey," Aunt Ginnie said, pressing a shot glass into Edgar's hand. "Here, take a sip."

He gulped the liquid down and scrunched his nose.

"That's gross."

Aunt Ginnie smiled. She uncorked the whiskey bottle on the tray and poured herself another shot.

Edgar finished his story and felt unburdened at the end of the telling.

"Your story is incredible, and I believe you. I really do," Aunt Ginnie said, wiping a drop of whiskey from her lips. "You sound like Sol, you know? He insists these creatures existed. It says they looked like insects, but I would never have guessed praying mantises, not from the translation."

Aunt Ginnie shook her head in disbelief. "And you can see them too, Clara?" Before Clara could answer, Aunt Ginnie puttered back into the kitchen.

Edgar heard the wet squeak of a cork being pulled from a bottle.

"The text said only a handful of humans could see these creatures after they were banished," Aunt Ginnie said, walking back into the room. "They had a type of second sight. Seers is what I think these special folks were called."

Aunt Ginnie's hands cupped her mouth.

"You're a Seer," she said, the words flowing through laced fingers.

"What do you mean, a Seer?" Edgar asked.

Aunt Ginnie opened the book back up to a photograph of one of the clay tablets.

"The story says that after the Phantids were banished, they did come back, but they weren't able to interact with humans anymore. Not in the same way. They could only hunt the ghosts of the dead. And the only thing in their way were Seers, humans who could see these demons and the recently departed."

"So the Seers and the Striders fought?" Edgar asked.

"Yes, Seers slayed the demons and helped the dead find their way to the afterlife."

"How'd they fight them?" Edgar asked, moving his head closer to the book.

Aunt Ginnie smiled and pointed to the last few lines on the page she was reading. The translation read, the Ash of Edom.

CHAPTER 23
THE ASH OF EDOM

"Salt, charcoal, and . . ." Edgar's eyes bulged as he read the recipe's final ingredient out loud. ". . . crushed human bone?"

The last three words came out more as an exclamation than a question. He slammed the book shut. "Dead people! That's what the Ash of Edom is made of?"

"Equal portions of all three elements, to be exact." Aunt Ginnie giggled as she shoved a stack of cardboard boxes blocking a corner curio in the living room. "I've always wanted to make it."

Edgar ran a hand through his hair. This was getting too weird, even for him. "Where the heck are we going to get bones—a graveyard?" He laughed at his own question, but saw the corners of Clara's lips curl into a devilish smile.

Only one person in the world could convince him to dig up a corpse and he was staring into her wild, brown eyes. *I bet she's already done this sort of thing*, he thought.

"I'm down for that!" she said, pumping her fists in the air.

Edgar blew a gust of air from his mouth. He imagined being caught by the police, waist-deep in a grave with a shovel held over his head, and the inevitable news head-line flashing across every smartphone in the neighbor-hood: Edgar "Tombstone" Tooms Caught Desecrating Local Cemetery.

He shook the images away. "No way! It's too risky."

"Calm down, you two. No one's going grave robbing. All we need to do is raid my private ossuary collection." Aunt Ginnie opened the curio's wooden doors, revealing a collection of human skulls and long femurs sitting on two dusty shelves. "Ta-da!"

"Holy crap!" Edgar and Clara said in unison. Charles frowned as he stared into the hollow sockets of one of the long departed.

"What? It's not like I killed them. Owning remains like this is perfectly legal." Aunt Ginnie placed a palm on one of the skulls. It was so old and desiccated that her fingers plunged through the cranium's temples. Then the skull collapsed in on itself like a sandcastle. "We'll have no trouble turning these into powder."

Edgar and Clara watched her assemble a few tools: a large stone mortar and pestle from the cabinet, a hammer, ziplock bags from a drawer by the refrigerator, safety goggles hanging above the sink, and a few charcoal briquettes from a bag in the kitchen's mudroom.

"Can you really make the powder?" Edgar asked.

"You bet! Just give me a little bit and I can whip up a few pouches. Why don't you two go back to the living room and read more of that book? And feel free to get cozy," she said with a wink.

Edgar turned to Clara. "She knows we're not a couple, right?"

Clara rolled her eyes and walked back to the couch.

He looked up at Opa. "What? Did I say something wrong?"

His grandfather laughed and zipped ahead. Edgar shrugged his shoulders and followed.

CHAPTER 24
TAKING NOTES

The sound of bones cracking and splintering faded as Edgar lost himself within the yellowed pages of *The Forgotten Gods of the Ancient Akkadian Empire*. Clara sat next to him, looking equally absorbed, while Opa Chuck hovered above them both.

Edgar moaned occasionally, learning new and horrific details about the creature he fought off. Striders, he read, were powerful demons immune to human weapons.

If the mantis returned, would he be able to protect his grandfather again? And what if more than one showed up? What then? Dozens of questions raced through his mind until Opa Chuck materialized through the book.

"Could one of you please say something? I can't focus on these tiny letters from up there." He inched out from the book and floated toward the center of the room. "That beast almost ate me, and I want to suss out how to fight back—pronto!"

Edgar had never heard his grandfather's voice crack before. He sounded scared.

"Sorry, Opa," Edgar said. "We just got into it. All of this is so weird and creepy."

"Yeah, listen to this." Clara tapped the page. "The author says that these demons are stronger than a Syrian elephant and faster than lions. And that in a fight, it wasn't uncommon to lose five Seers for every Strider killed."

"Those are horrible odds," Edgar said.

"Turn to page 147!" Aunt Ginnie shouted from the kitchen.

"Why?" Clara yelled.

Aunt Ginnie stepped out of the kitchen. Her hair, face, and clothing were coated with a thin layer of grayish powder. "Ay, niña! Don't you want to learn how to turn these monsters into a steaming pile of goo?"

Clara's eyes quivered with excitement. She ripped the book from Edgar's hands. She found the page and read the passage aloud:

"Seers in Ancient Mesopotamia used the Ash of Edom as a defensive and offensive weapon. It could be sprinkled around the home to prevent Striders from entering to collect the souls of the recently departed. As a weapon, the Ash was blown onto a Phantid's armored skin through long reeds. The mixture, in correct proportions, dissolved the creature's thick shells and boiled them alive. In lower concentrations, the Ash of Edom stopped Striders from using their powers.

"Powers? What kind of powers?" Edgar asked.

"Teleportation, flight, shape-shifting, mesmerism, and, oh, this is bad . . ." Clara turned the page. ". . . the ability to breathe out poison gas."

"That must be the black cloud that giant bug disappeared into!" Edgar said.

Aunt Ginnie poked her head out from the doorway. "My God, you saw pneuma?"

"New-mah?" Edgar repeated. "I don't know if it's the same thing, but Opa and I saw it blow out a black cloud from its mouth. I don't think it was poisonous though. It didn't hurt us."

"That's amazing, Edgar," Aunt Ginnie said, shaking her head. A gray halo erupted around her hair. "I believe that pneuma, the black cloud you saw, is the physical manifestation of their magical powers."

"Why's she so excited about this?" Opa Chuck asked, as Aunt Ginnie disappeared into the kitchen again. "She wouldn't think it was so great if she was being chased by—"

"Voila, they're done!" Aunt Ginnie said, walking into the room. She held three sandwich-sized ziplock bags bulging with Ash above her head. The coarse powder was gray and spotted with shards of charcoal.

"Tía, you made three bags?" Clara asked.

Aunt Ginnie smiled. "Yeah, one for each of you and an extra one . . . for me."

"You're coming to help us?" Edgar asked.

"Of course! Anything for my Clara. Besides, do you know how long I've studied the Forgotten Gods?" Ginnie took the book from Clara's hands and pressed it to her chest. "Now I have a chance to see these myths in real life."

"Wait, how are you going to do that?" Edgar asked.

"Well, if you were able to share your vision with Clara, don't you think it would work for me?" Aunt Ginnie asked.

"We could try," Edgar said, glancing toward Clara who nodded her head.

"Great! Will we need candles?" Aunt Ginnie asked.

CHAPTER 25
AN OLD-TIMEY SEANCE

Ginnie watched Edgar and Clara talk in the living room as she arranged papers on the dining room table. They'd asked for a few minutes alone to strategize how to reveal Edgar's grandfather. Occasionally, they'd defer a question to the space between them, Charles Tooms apparently.

The boy is strange, Ginnie thought, but Clara was one of the most astute judges of character Ginnie ever met—far wiser than her twelve years—and if Edgar was her best friend, then he was ok in her book. But she couldn't shake the suspicion that this was an elaborate practical joke.

I'm going to beat that girl back into her momma if this is a prank, she thought. But there was no reason, beyond run-of-the-mill paranoia, that she should suspect anything weird. Well, anything weirder than Edgar's story.

Was it so strange? she wondered. Any stranger than Inanna's Descent to the Netherworld, Lamassu's Lament, or the Epic of Gilgamesh? History was full of stories with gods, creatures, and just like Edgar's story, demons.

Ginnie looked over at a picture of Sol in the kitchen

and wondered what he would think of Edgar's story. He'd approve of the little experiment they were about to embark on.

"Are you ready?" Clara asked, motioning for Ginnie to join them in the living room.

"Yes, of course." Ginnie touched Sol's picture before joining her niece.

Ginnie looked down at Clara's smiling face on her left and Edgar's determined face on her right.

"Opa's all set," Edgar said. "Gramps is here, in the center of the circle. Are you ready, Mrs. Ginnie?"

"You can call me Aunt Ginnie if you want, Edgar." Ginnie joined the circle and shimmied in place. "This is exciting! Like an old-timey seance."

Ginnie extended her hand and Edgar squeezed.

"Ah!" Ginnie shouted.

"What? You see him already?"

"No, you cracked my fingers. Let's try again."

They held hands again.

"Anything?" Edgar asked, loosening his grip.

"No, I'm sorry," Ginnie said.

In the center of the circle, Charles shook his head and drifted toward his grandson.

"It's ok, kiddo. At least we tried," Charles said, taking a spot just above Edgar's right shoulder.

Ginnie gasped. "Who said that?"

Edgar and Clara looked at each other. Charles floated toward Ginnie. "Professor Diaz? Can you hear me?"

"Yes! Yes! I can hear you!" Ginnie shouted, looking all around the room.

Edgar, Clara, and Charles cheered.

"We're so close! What if we all held hands?" Clara said.

Edgar shrugged his shoulders. "Couldn't hurt."

When they connected the circle, Ginnie let go immediately and stepped backward.

"I saw a balloon . . . there," she said, pointing a trembling finger.

"That wasn't a balloon," Edgar said. "That's Opa Chuck. Come on. We can do this."

Ginnie shuffled back toward the children, closed her eyes, and let Edgar grab her hand again. An electric tingle crawled through her skin. She opened her eyes and came face-to-face with Charles Tooms's bobbing face.

"¡Hijo de puta!"

"Excuse me?" Charles asked.

Ginnie laughed and covered her mouth. "I'm so sorry! I didn't mean to call you that. It's just that—" She looked at Clara and then at Edgar. "Is this really happening? Am I talking to a floating head, or did I just have a stroke?"

"Oh, this is happening," Charles said hovering closer.

Ginnie laughed and held Clara in front of her like a shield.

"You're real, aren't you?" Ginnie asked.

"Yup."

"And you're dead."

"Correct again. Someone give the young lady a prize," Charles said.

"Opa!"

Charles smiled. "I'm sorry. Just trying to liven the mood. This is a shock to me too. No one besides Edgar and Clara have been able to see me. You two are the first human beings I've talked to in eleven years."

"I have so many questions," Ginnie said.

"You and me both. But I have one that needs answering

right away. Do we really have a shot at beating these creatures with this . . ." Charles's chin jutted toward the bag of Ash in Ginnie's hand. ". . . Ash of Edom stuff?"

"Honestly, I have no idea, but it's all we have," Ginnie said.

Charles frowned. "Well, I appreciate the honesty."

Edgar's cell phone buzzed. Ginnie saw that he silenced the call. A moment later, the electronic tablet rumbled in his pocket again.

"You should take that if it's important, Edgar," Ginnie said.

"It's my mom," he said, looking around.

Clara punched him in the shoulder. "Take it, dummy!"

Edgar answered and put the call on speaker.

"Edgar! Get your butt back home this instant," Margaret shouted through the speaker.

"Mom, what's going on?"

"Cockroaches! We've got a roach infestation all over the house!"

"Ok, we'll be right there." Edgar tapped the red phone icon.

"It's them," Charles said, zipping around the trio. "The fuckers are back."

"Language!" Edgar said, grinning.

"Come on. I'll drive you all there," Ginnie said.

"Are you sure?" Edgar said.

"I wouldn't miss this for the world!" Ginnie said, gathering her purse and the ziplock bags full of Ash.

CHAPTER 26
INFESTATION

Edgar caught a glimpse of his mother through a side window swinging a broom at an unseen assailant as Aunt Ginnie pulled into the driveway. Her last wild swoop connected with a ceiling fan, sending flecks of plaster and electrical sparks raining down atop her head.

"Stay in the car, everyone," he said, jumping out the passenger side and rushing toward the front door.

If Andrés was back, he couldn't chance letting him near Opa Chuck. He fought it once before and he was certain he could do it again thanks to the protection powder Aunt Ginnie had made. He patted his bulging pocket as he ran toward the house, puffs of white trailed behind him.

Edgar opened the front door and his mother yelled, "DIE!"

Glass shattered somewhere in the house. The sound of destruction was followed by a series of thumps from upstairs and the sound of furniture overturning.

"Got you, you dirty bastards!" he heard her yell.

Edgar ran up the stairs, but the sound of squelching underfoot stopped him. Smears of crushed cockroaches covered the steps. A few continued to writhe with what was left of their segmented bodies. The sight was nauseating. His stomach churned and Edgar felt dizzy as he struggled to balance himself.

"Edgar? Is that you?" he heard his mother ask.

He responded by retching on the stairs, coating an unscathed mass of bugs with viscous vomit that smelled of whiskey. He watched the cockroaches wade through the muck, antennae dripping with throw up the color of hardened tallow.

"It's me, Mom . . . it's me," Edgar mumbled, heaving twice again over the railing. The vomit pattered on the floorboards below. He steadied himself and shook off the warm spittle and the handful of roaches that crawled up his arm. He ran up the stairs, ignoring the squishing sounds his shoes made with every step.

"In here!" his mother said, poking her head out of the master bedroom.

Edgar walked in and clasped a hand over his mouth. The stairs were disgusting, but the sight in front of him made his head hurt—beetles, ants, centipedes, and spiders joined the cockroaches to form throbbing, muddy veins that pulsed along the walls.

"Edgar, what's happening to our house?" his mother asked, throwing the broom down.

He suspected that this infestation was the work of the giant green mantis, but how could he explain to his mother that ancient bug demons were crossing over to hunt the ghost of his grandfather?

She looked over to Edgar and frowned. "Jesus. You look pale, Edgar. What is that smell? Have you been—"

"Hello? Can we come in?" a voice asked.

"Who's downstairs?"

"Aunt Ginnie."

"Who the hell is Aunt Ginnie?"

CHAPTER 27
BUG CONTROL

Edgar held the banister with one hand and shooed away clouds of insects thrumming through the air with the other as he slowly made his way back down the stairs with his mother following close behind.

Tiny claws and legs crawled and picked at his skin. All he wanted to do was find a clean, bug-free room and take a shower.

"Watch your step, Mom. It's slippery. There are dead roaches everywhere and—"

"They're crawling on the walls too!" Margaret cried. "I can't believe you brought someone over, Edgar. The house is disgusting!"

"They're just here to help."

He could feel his mother's eyes roll into her skull.

"Oh, is your girlfriend a professional exterminator now?"

"Why is everyone so obsessed with my relationship with Clara? She's not my—"

Clara cleared her throat.

Edgar was so focused on where to put his next step that he hadn't seen Clara, Aunt Ginnie, and Opa Chuck at the bottom of the stairs.

"We're just friends, Mrs. Tooms," Clara said, crossing her arms.

Why'd she cross her arms like that? Was she mad at him?

Margaret pushed Edgar aside and glared at her visitors. Puffs of flying gnats flew between them like tumbleweeds.

This isn't going to go well, Edgar thought. He could feel the anger radiate from her impish frame as Aunt Ginnie extended her hand.

Edgar's eyes widened as his mom crossed her arms. He noticed Clara's equally startled reaction and hoped to God that she wouldn't lose her cool.

"What's going on?" Clara mouthed.

"Margaret hates unannounced visitors," Opa Chuck whispered as he hovered between the two families. He rose to Aunt Ginnie's height. "She also hates an untidy house and, oh, boy, is it a mess today. One of you better say something."

Thank goodness for Opa Chuck, Edgar thought.

Aunt Ginnie stepped forward and laid her palms over her heart.

"Mrs. Tooms? Hi, I'm Ginevra Diaz, Director of NYU's Center for Ancient Studies. It's a pleasure to meet you."

Edgar coughed and jabbed Clara with his elbow.

"This is my aunt, Mrs. Tooms," Clara said.

This extra bit of information seemed to soften his mother's defiance. Her frown straightened into a dagger-thin smile.

Edgar felt her gaze turn toward him. "Honey, I told

you there was a roach infestation. Why in the world would you bring company over?"

Edgar stared at his shoes. What could he say? Mom, I thought you were going to be murdered by giant praying mantises, so I brought over some help and this protection powder. She wouldn't believe him.

"Oh, it's ok, Mrs. Tooms," Aunt Ginnie said. "Clara and I are amateur entomologists. Infestations like this are very rare and we just wanted to see if we could help, that's all."

"Can you?" Margaret asked.

"What?" Aunt Ginnie said.

"Help. With this?" Margaret clarified, waving her arms at the chittering insects crawling over the floors and walls.

Ginnie smiled and swung her purse around. As her hands rooted through the contents, the plastic bag of Ash she was looking for toppled out and fell to the floor. The white dust spilled out and coated the carpet. The insects scattered into every available crack and crevice.

Margaret hopped on one leg as a stream of beetles scuttled past her. "What in the world is in that bag?" Margaret asked, staring in disbelief at the retreating bugs.

"Oh, just some salt and hum—"

"HUM-ungous amounts of boric acid!" Clara said, stepping in front of her aunt. "It's a Diaz family recipe."

Margaret embraced Clara and kissed the top of her head. "Well, thank you both for whatever's in that bag. I thought we were going to have to move out." She let go of Clara and glanced at the ceiling. "Do you mind if we spread some of that stuff upstairs?"

"I was just going to suggest that," Aunt Ginnie said,

bending over to scoop up some of the powder back into the plastic.

Edgar reached for the bag in his back pocket to share, but Aunt Ginnie shook her head.

"She's right, kiddo. You need to stay armed," Opa Chuck said. "We don't have much of that stuff to go around."

Opa was right. Edgar watched the two adults pad up the stairs and smiled as he heard his mother say, "I love your bracelets by the way."

"Ok, that went better than expected," he said.

"Yeah, I thought your mom was going to lose it and kick us out," Clara said.

"Well, now that they're upstairs, the two of you should start spreading the powder on the windowsills and in front of all the doors like in the book," Opa Chuck said. He turned his attention to the floor. "Did anyone hear that?"

"Hear what?" Clara asked.

Opa Chuck whirled around his grandson's head. "It sounds like something's in the basement. Something big."

"Stop doing that, Opa!" Edgar pleaded, swiping at his grandfather. "You're making me nervous!"

"Well, we should be if those monsters are back."

"How can we be sure?" Clara asked.

Just as Clara finished her question, a gust of icy air rushed through the house, chilling Edgar to the bone. Clara hugged herself and started shaking.

"Did you guys feel that?" Opa Chuck asked.

Edgar nodded as his mother and Aunt Ginnie shrieked from the second floor. The cold front had traveled up the stairs.

"This is how it happened," Opa Chuck said. "First the cold and then the glow."

"What glow?" Clara asked, teeth chattering.

"Opa said the house glowed blue when Andrés first appeared."

"No, it was more like the house was sweating color, not just glowing."

Edgar jumped backward. "It's happening again." He pointed at the floor where pools of thick, purple light burbled out from between the floorboards and spread like taffy.

"Everyone, get your bags ready. The beast is back," Opa Chuck whispered.

CHAPTER 28
PINCER MOVE

Malva loved human basements.

The dampness in the air and the rough concrete floor reminded her of the Rookery. She licked the smooth outer curves of her sickle-shaped forelimbs with her human tongue, running it back and forth until streams of spittle flowed over the chitinous casings.

"Do you have to clean yourself like that?" Andrés asked, cocking his head to the side. "I'm sure you've wiped off all the fungus from the teleportation. You've been at it for—"

Malva flicked her claws open like butterfly knives, revealing rows of thorny spikes. The motion sent Andrés stumbling backward, knocking over a child's wooden rocking horse. Its garishly colored head snapped in half on the floor.

"Gods below!" Andrés snapped, scrambling to right himself. "We made it into the basement without the boy and the ghost hearing us and you just gave away our position."

He wasn't wrong, but Malva wasn't about to admit to the mistake. She cleared her mind. She realized that this newfound compulsion to clean didn't stem from fastidiousness, but from anxiety that they were about to face the first Seer in over two thousand years.

The weight of this confrontation flared in her mind the moment she stepped out of the teleportation cloud. She had gleefully accepted the assignment from her uncle, but now that she was in Eperu, just a few hundred feet from the boy, she was unsure her talents would be enough to win out.

But Edgar Tooms was a small human child. Untrained to boot. How much damage could he possibly do?

Malva snuck a look at Andrés's wounded claw and stared at the answer.

Could the same or worse happen to her?

"If you must know, it was painful," Andrés said, following her gaze. He covered the concave blemish with his other claw. "The boy's hand burned through my shell as he squeezed. It was excruciating."

"At least he's not in control of all of his powers."

"You're right. I've heard the stories. Seers could peel off exoskeletons with a chant and hand gesture, couldn't they?"

Malva nodded. "They were gifted humans, but they're gone now. Let's make sure this one doesn't get any older or breed with the girl," Malva growled, feeling her old self return. She looked up at the sheetrock a few inches above their head. "Can you fly?"

"Yes, of course."

"Through the walls and ceilings?"

Andrés raised his claws; they passed easily through the

paneling and timber above their heads. Malva exhaled a black cloud of relief. There was something about the Tooms' home that made their ability to stay unseen or pass through objects difficult. She was glad to see Andrés was in control of his powers.

"Good. Head to the boy's room. See if the ghost is up there. I'll check the bottom floors for the Seer. We'll push them toward each other as planned."

Andrés nodded and shot up through the house. Malva sighed. *Wings were wasted on males*, she thought, as she crawled up the basement stairs. Malva stopped at the exit and for the first time in decades, felt a pang of fear.

She looked down at her body and imagined what it would be like to be flayed alive, to feel her exoskeleton ripped apart, plate by plate, and see the strings of muscle and tissue snap, leaving behind jiggling white meat. It would be a horrible way to die.

No! she thought. She was the Ghost Scythe—the one who brought death to the dead.

Malva shook the thought of her own demise away, sealed the segments around her human mouth shut, and marched through the door into the Tooms' family home.

CHAPTER 29
THE HUNTERS ARRIVE

Edgar gazed at the ceiling. Motes of plaster dust floated down and the house shook like the second floor was overrun with wild horses. He was about to ask Opa Chuck and Clara if they heard the commotion, but Aunt Ginnie's flustered voice turned his attention back toward the entrance. He rushed to the source with Clara and Opa Chuck close behind.

"Ay Dios mío! Ay Dios mío!" Ginnie shouted, running down the stairs. She jumped the final three steps, nearly colliding with the children as she reached the landing.

"There's a giant praying mantis coming down from the attic," she yelled, scooping Edgar and Clara into her arms. "Your mom couldn't see or hear it."

"Ginevra! Are you ok?" Margaret asked from upstairs.

"Um, yes?" Aunt Ginnie's eyes darted frantically around the house.

"You don't sound ok. I'll be right down. Is Edgar there with you?"

"I'm here, Mom," Edgar said, slipping out from Aunt Ginnie's grasp.

"Ok, good. Try to calm Mrs. Diaz down, alright? I'll be right there."

Edgar and Clara held Aunt Ginnie's hands as she struggled to breathe.

"Ginnie, look at me," Charles said. "Take a deep breath and let it out slowly."

She nodded and followed his instructions. Charles rose to the ceiling as Aunt Ginnie inhaled and descended as she exhaled. He repeated this until her breathing settled.

"Opa, you're a genius!" Edgar watched Aunt Ginnie recover from the shock of seeing the Strider upstairs. For a moment, Edgar thought she'd be ok, but the stairs creaked, and Aunt Ginnie's rasping breath returned.

"It's coming," she whispered.

The four looked up, expecting to see long, spiked insect legs, but instead Margaret's slipper-clad feet made their way down.

"It's you, Mrs. Tooms!" Aunt Ginnie exhaled.

"Of course it's me. What in the world happened? One minute we were chatting and the next you froze like you saw a—"

Margaret's eyes widened as floorboards above their head groaned. Margaret turned to walk up and paused as the second-floor stairs creaked. The noises suddenly stopped, and Margaret shrugged her shoulders.

"God, that's embarrassing. These old houses, always expanding with the heat," Margaret said with a smile. She turned once more toward the stairs and then back to the trio. "Ginevra, I'm going to make you some tea, ok?"

"That'll be lovely," Aunt Ginnie said. Once out of

earshot, she turned toward Edgar and grabbed him by the shoulders. "It's upstairs. It's huge!" she said.

"I have to call Sol," Aunt Ginnie said, taking out her cell phone. The call went straight to voicemail.

"Sol? Sol! They're real. Phantids are real! I just saw one at 234 Warburton Avenue in Dobbs Ferry, New York. My niece's boyfriend, Edgar Tooms, can see them. He, um, shared his vision with me. Sol, you better get down here," Aunt Ginnie said.

Clara tugged at her aunt's kaftan.

"What?"

"Edgar's not my boyfriend. We're just friends," Clara said.

"Best friends." Edgar shuffled closer.

"Isn't that sweet?" a voice asked.

The group looked at each other, unsure of where the voice was coming from.

"Won't you join me in the living room?" the voice asked again.

"That must be the other one," Edgar said. "The big one."

CHAPTER 30

PEEP SHOW

Turning the corner, Edgar saw Malva crouched in the center of the living room. Her forelimbs and legs were pulled close to her body, making her look like an alabaster column bristling with purple flower petals.

Behind them, Andrés thundered down the stairs. He leaped over the railing and landed with a thud that reverberated throughout the house.

"Little ghost, it's time to go," Andrés said, knocking his claws together. The thumping sounded like two hollow logs.

Aunt Ginnie trembled and placed a hand on Edgar's shoulder.

"Is this really happening?" she asked.

"It'll be ok. Just stay behind me," he said, taking a few steps back into the living room, eager to put more space between himself and Andrés who was skulking closer.

Edgar turned his attention back to Malva—her head was pointed at him, but he couldn't be sure she was staring at him. Indigo smudges ran down her lavender tinted, tear-shaped eyes. Just beneath the smudges, a dark purple square clambered up and down the length of each eye. Their jagged movements reminded Edgar of a horseshoe crab scuttling through sand against a strong tide. He shivered at the idea of a creature living inside an eyeball.

The boxes suddenly slowed and froze in place near the top of her eyes as he stepped closer.

"Who are you and what do you want?" Edgar asked, crossing his arms. He hoped the gesture made him look tougher than he felt.

"I'm Malva, my love. We've come for the head," she said, as the plates around her beakish jaw twitched. Edgar flinched as the plating suddenly folded back like crinkled aluminum foil, revealing a pitch-black hole between her outstretched mandibles. What looked like the lower half of a porcelain doll's face emerged from the shadow and smiled.

"You're different. You're a girl?" Edgar asked, startled by the sight of Malva's delicate, human face.

"Would you like me to be?" Malva licked her pale lips. "I can be a woman for you."

The furniture shook as she let her abdomen slap the ground. The leathery segments throbbed while her long antennae fluttered.

Malva threw her head back and spread her sinewy forelimbs out. The pose reminded Edgar of the crucifixes decorating Clara's house.

"Madre de Dios," Aunt Ginnie whispered.

"Just watch and enjoy the show." Malva threw her head back and inhaled deeply. Two domes bulged out from the center of Malva's pale chest. The thick armor plating thinned around the engorged curves, cracking and flaking off, revealing patches of smooth human skin.

Malva chittered and caressed her growing bosom with the spiked end of her left claw. "Are you enjoying the show, boy? I can make them as big as you like."

The smell of cinnamon suddenly blanketed the room. Edgar gagged as the aroma wriggled into his nose and down his throat. Clara and Aunt Ginnie both doubled over and grabbed their knees while dry heaving. Even Opa Chuck gasped for air. Liquid rumbled inside Malva's body.

Malva groaned with pleasure as her new glands engorged, and with a loud pop, nipples emerged from each breast.

Sweat beaded on Edgar's forehead as waves of throbbing heat consumed his body. The corners of his mouth curled into a trembling smile.

Malva cackled. "Someone wants to see more."

Edgar shook his head and clasped a hand over his mouth. He didn't want Malva or anyone else to know, but the truth was, he wanted Malva to continue. Shame washed over him, and he fell to his knees. *What else could she show him?* he wondered.

The bizarre scene in front of him darkened and from a sharp, defiant voice rose somewhere in the room, "Stop it! Stop doing that to him!"

Was that Clara? All he could see was her wavy red hair as she stepped in front of him.

"I said stop it!" she yelled again, reaching into her cargo pockets.

Malva reared up on her legs and hissed like a cat.

"What's in your pocket, girl? Don't you know that you can't—"

Before Malva could finish, a white cloud bloomed from Clara's hands and coated the creature's face. Malva shrieked as the bone dust on her face turned to a thick, bubbling paste.

"It burns!" Malva screamed, furiously scraping at her eyes. As she scraped, her claw snapped off an antenna.

"Throw some more on her, Clara! Kill it!" Aunt Ginnie shouted.

Malva roared and charged forward. Clara and Edgar jumped away, but Malva knocked Aunt Ginnie on her back.

Aunt Ginnie crawled toward the couch and hugged her ribs.

Malva paced the room, jabbing at the air like a drunk boxer, but she collapsed with every step. In a last-ditch effort to balance herself, Malva's legs splayed outward and clamped down on anything solid, including Aunt Ginnie's foot.

Clara's aunt howled as she tugged at the pale appendage pinning her to the ground. As Aunt Ginnie grasped the glistening leg, Malva's swinging arms knocked her unconscious.

"Tía!" Clara screamed, taking a step forward, but Edgar held her back.

"It's too dangerous to get near them. Look, even the other Strider is staying away." Edgar pointed at Andrés who had backed into a far corner.

"Andrés!" Malva managed to gasp in between heaves, slurring her words. "Where are you? Do something!"

The green mantis seemed just as scared as they were

and appeared to be avoiding the mushy black lumps oozing from Malva's mouth. The smell of burned rosemary filled the air as the puddles sizzled on the carpet.

"Don't get close to that stuff!" Opa Chuck yelled, circling the room. Edgar stepped backward, pulling Clara with him.

They halted their retreat as Margaret walked into the living room carrying a tray of filled teacups.

"What's all this commotion about?" she asked, maneuvering around the children. She dropped the tray at the sight of Aunt Ginnie's body on the floor.

"What did you kids do to her?" Margaret shouted. "I told you to try and calm Mrs. Diaz down. What the hell happened?"

Edgar grabbed his mother's wrist and spun her around.

"Mom, you need to see, really see!" Edgar said, nodding toward the space where Malva flailed.

She tried to wrench her arm free, but couldn't shake Edgar's grip.

It was time for her to see, Edgar thought. He gripped her tighter and concentrated, trying to send a charged current from his body into hers. Edgar felt her resistance slacken and looked up.

"Can you see the—"

Margaret's right hand smacked him across the cheek. Everyone in the room, including Andrés, gasped.

"Let go of me, young man. You need to stop this right now, Edgar Ezekiel Tooms. Whatever game this is, please stop," Margaret said, tears welling up in her eyes. "Please let go."

"Look!" Edgar said, finally sending a wave of electricity surging between their hands.

Margaret stumbled backward. Edgar watched as she focused her gaze where Malva dug her legs into Aunt Ginnie and the floor. She could see! Why else would she bury the heels of her hands into her eyes?

"Mom! Calm down. Please, calm down. You need to see what we're seeing. You have no idea how much danger we're in."

"Edgar! Watch out!" Charles shouted, as black vapor billowed out of Andrés's mouth. The cloud extended its smokey tendrils around the room.

Margaret dropped her hands and looked up. "Dad? Is that you?"

"Margie, before you scream, just know that I love you." Charles gave her his best smile.

Margaret shook her head and clasped her mouth with both hands as she stepped backward.

"This . . . isn't real," she said in between heaving breaths.

"Mom, you need to sit down," Edgar said, grasping his mother by her shoulders.

Margaret screamed at his touch and toppled over like a freshly cut Christmas pine, her head bounced on the floor with a hollow thud. Clara rushed to Margaret's side and Charles hovered above his daughter.

Edgar turned to see the black smoke retreat and condense over Malva as she squatted on the floor. Andrés extended his claw and fresh wisps of smoke slithered over him. The black smoke covered their bodies and the black forms softened and wobbled like a mirage.

The cloud burst, sending out a shockwave that

knocked everyone in the room onto their backs, and in Charles's case, through a wall. All that remained of the two creatures was a growing puddle of black ooze and a dark stain running up the wall and ceiling.

Edgar patted his body and looked around the room. His mother was passed out on the rug. Opa Chuck zipped past Edgar toward Clara, sobbing on her knees.

"Clara, are you ok?" Charles asked. "What happened?"

"Aunt Ginnie's gone," she said, pointing toward the darkened spot. "I saw her get sucked into that cloud."

CHAPTER 31
GINNIE'S VOICEMAIL

Sol Balam stared at his cell phone.

Ginnie's strange voicemail made two things clear: Phantids walked among the living again and there was a new Seer in the world.

Could it be true?

He had no reason to believe Ginnie was lying. There'd be no point. No, she was frantic, genuinely shaken, as if she'd seen the creatures herself.

Sol hissed through clenched teeth. *There'd be no shaking that vision from one's head*, he thought.

Sol ran a hand over his smooth scalp. The last recorded Seer died thousands of years ago, and if this Edgar Tooms could actually see Phantids, then he was probably in danger. From his own experience, he knew that these creatures would do anything to keep their existence hidden from the world.

It would take him an hour by car to get to Dobbs Ferry, but something told him that he should get there sooner. That meant using unconventional travel methods.

He stared at two clay tablets resting on his desk. He ran a finger over the lines of cuneiform carved along their slightly curved surfaces. He picked up the largest, the size of a small paperback, and slipped it into the padded pocket of his leather briefcase.

Sol clutched the smaller tablet and pressed it to his forehead. "We had to use you someday, little one."

He walked over to his bedroom closet door, opened it, took a deep breath, and walked through the darkened threshold.

CHAPTER 32
THE MACE

"Psst! Ginevra, over here! Over here!"

Slumped against a stone wall, Ginnie heard the voice whispering from somewhere to the left, but she refused to turn her gaze from the bizarre scene in front of her—three giant praying mantises arguing.

She recognized the two from the living room, but not the bone-white juggernaut yelling and waving its sickle-shaped claws in the air. Spit and strange plumes of black smoke erupted from its clattering mandibles as it roared and circled the smaller creatures on four legs that resembled medieval spears. As it stomped, its strange, three-clawed feet slapped the floor tiles, sending sharp, percussive waves through Ginnie's numb body.

The one that looked as if it was fringed with orchid petals dropped its head and said, "No, my Marquis!"

Was that the big one's name, title, or both? That didn't matter. The creatures were distracted and that presented an opportunity to get away from this nightmare.

Ginnie tried to push further up against the wall but

couldn't lift her arms. Something heavy pinned them to the ground. She glanced down, expecting to see old-fashioned iron manacles, but instead caught sight of her deformed hands spread across the stone floor.

Engorged to five times their size, the skin spread so taut around new layers of fat that the slightest pinprick would have popped them apart. She shuddered at the thought.

Ginnie clenched her hands into fists. Her sausage fingers slowly curled inward, biting into the meat of her puffy palms. She raised her fists and grinned. All she needed was a gigantic, white glove and her hands would resemble Goofy's—her favorite Disney character. Her smile disappeared as she realized that her arms were little more than flesh-colored tubes.

"What the hell happened to me," she muttered, sneaking a glance down. Whatever happened to her hands had worked its magic on the rest of her body, causing it to deform into cartoonish proportions.

Her swollen feet were attached to legs thin as pipe stems. Her pear-shaped abdomen heaved up and down as she struggled to breathe. Ginnie cupped the two domes centered on her chest with her enormous palms. Like the rest of her body, they were as smooth as a cue ball.

"I'm a freak," she whispered.

Ginnie traced the outline of her head with trembling fingertips. It felt more like a beach ball than a skull. She closed her eyes and shook her head. Her hair crackled in the air as if on fire.

"Ah, yes, you've noticed that your body's a little . . . different. You're in the underworld, my dear, and you're not dead. Something had to change," the voice from earlier said.

Ginnie turned her head to face the source, but all she could see were giant orchid petals and an enormous staff leaning against the wall. It was a long iron rod as thick as a flagpole and capped with a beautifully cast ox head, its pupils and bridle outlined in sparkling gold.

A string of smoke billowed from its cavernous nostrils and its eyes winked. It happened so fast that Ginnie thought she had imagined the movements, but then it batted its eyes again.

"Jesus fucking Christ!" Ginnie shouted, recoiling and banging her globular head against the wall.

"Don't be so dramatic," the staff said, shifting its weight so it stood perfectly straight. "You'll need my help if you want to get out of here."

"What the hell are you?"

"My name is Sharur, the—"

"Smasher of Thousands?"

The staff smiled. "You know of me?"

"Of course! You helped Ninurta defeat Asag! Set fire to mountains, demolished legions of rock demons, birthed hurricanes—you're a legend! Literally a legend," Ginnie said, narrowing her now disk-like eyes. "How's this possible? You shouldn't be real."

"Oh, Ginevra, I assure you that I am very real, and I am flattered. How is it that my exploits are still sung in Eperu?"

"Eperu? Earth. The living Earth? Well, they're not. Not really. I'm a professor and one of my specialties is Sumerian mythology," Ginnie paused. "Wait, how do you know my name?"

"Ah, that's easy. I can read the minds of any human being that wanders here."

"Where is here and why do you want to help me?"

"Too many questions. Let's just say that I used to belong to a better class of, um, leader."

The staff wobbled on the tiled floor as the Marquis stomped closer.

"We'll need to continue this conversation later. I'm afraid my current master is about to turn his attention toward you now. Perhaps you should stay asleep for a bit longer, eh?"

Ginnie opened her mouth to protest, but the staff was quicker, and the last thing she saw was the ox head careening toward her forehead.

CHAPTER 33
REPERCUSSIONS

Andrés ducked under the Marquis's swing. His enormous claws whirred inches above his head.

This was the second time in as many days Andrés found himself cowering under the Marquis's glare. His master had been screaming for an hour and now launched into another round of recriminations.

"How could an experienced hunter and my niece—Malva, the Ghost Scythe—fail so spectacularly at the hands of children?" the Marquis boomed, his feathered antennae fluttering like torches.

Andrés raised a claw to speak.

"Don't you dare!" the Marquis shouted.

"Uncle, they had some of the Knowledge. The girl used the Ash of Edom. She nearly killed me," Malva argued, turning in a circle to show off splotches of bone dust and salt still clinging to her carapace.

"Excuses! Nothing but excuses! You should have gone with a coating of armored mites!"

Good, Andrés thought. *Let Malva take the brunt of her*

uncle's fury. It's not like the Marquis would listen to him or even acknowledge that his actions saved his niece. A retreat, no matter the reason, was always a loss in the Strider world.

"You've grown slow and complacent, my dear. You know as well as I do that there are still a few humans scattered in that world with an inkling of our history," the Marquis said, marching back to his throne. He picked up Sharur and pointed the ox head at Ginnie's body.

"And you bring back this? A human? Into our world? We can't even process this one into Qurdum in her condition." The Marquis spat. The sticky wad landed between Andrés and Malva. "Useless. The two of you are useless."

"But the boy," Andrés whispered.

"Yes. The boy. This Edgar Tooms is a different matter," the Marquis said. "We haven't encountered a Seer in centuries. Not like this one. He can share his gifts and that power could spread like a virus."

"What would happen then, Uncle?"

"We could lose our grip on the Rookery. Humans drove us out of their world once. They could do it again by coming here. Who knows what this boy is capable of. We'll need to send in more of our warriors to take care of the mess you two left behind." The Marquis faced the corner of the throne room.

"Luther!"

"My Lord?" The scorpion chittered, crawling out from his hole.

"Luther, get word to General Cressida to put together an assault team. My niece and Andrés are under her command." The Marquis turned to the two Striders. "Report to the general and do as she says. Leave no survivors. Fail again, and I'll turn you both into Qurdum."

Malva and Andrés bowed and scuttled toward the exit in silence. As they approached the double doors, the Marquis spoke once more.

"Malva?"

"Yes, Uncle?"

"You look ridiculous with one antenna."

CHAPTER 34
MISSED OPPORTUNITY

Luther gazed at Ginnie's unconscious body and snapped his claws repeatedly. He'd never touched a human being before and wasn't looking forward to the sensation.

Would his pincers slice through her thin, pale skin? Gods, how could these fragile creatures go through life without armor? Could they feel the rigid skeletons hidden within their bodies?

"Luther? What are you waiting for? I told you to pick that thing up!" the Marquis shouted, putting an end to the questions floating through his mind. He'd forgotten that his master was standing just a few feet away.

"Yes, my Lord," Luther said, slowly scooping up Ginnie's body. He fought the urge to snap down as her limp body tickled the sensory hairs studded over and within the grooves of his bulky claws.

He supported the back of her neck within the crook of his left claw and held the back of her knees with the right. She sagged between his arms like a wet cloth. It wasn't an ideal grip, but at least she'd stay in one piece this way.

"What should I do with her, my Lord?" Luther asked.

"Donate her to the zookeeper. I'm sure she'll be happy to have a new attraction for the nymphs to ogle and chew on. I've had enough of this for the day," the Marquis said, tossing Sharur onto the ground next to the Orchid Throne. The mace landed with a hollow, metallic hum. "I'll be at the brothels."

Luther waited until the Marquis's thundering footsteps faded completely before walking over to the mace. His own six feet tapped against the floor and echoed throughout the chamber. Luther looked at the mace lying on the floor, its eyes turned toward the wall.

"Sharur," Luther whispered, "I saw you talking to the human."

The mace levitated off the ground and faced the scorpion. The golden outlines of his eyes narrowed as they focused on Luther's bobbing stinger.

"Luther, you don't have to do this."

"You heard the Marquis, brother."

"I told the woman that I'd help her and—"

"And if you do, who do you think they'll suspect set her free? Me, that's who. A lowly Crawler. Even if the Marquis didn't believe that I did it, he'd still process me into Qurdum, just on principle."

"It doesn't have to be that way. We could escape with this woman. You've always wanted to leave the Rookery and be free again. We both have," Sharur said, hovering closer. "And now we have a way out with her."

"No. Sharur, please stop. My claws are tied. The Marquis asked me to send her to the menagerie and that's what I'm going to do."

"You're making a mistake, brother. This human is the best chance we've had at escape."

"And where would we even go? Eperu? How would we even survive up there? We'd need to get to one of the other worlds and that's impossible without one of the Marquis's travel tablets."

Steam rumbled from Sharur's nostrils.

"You know I'm right, my friend. I wish to the Gods that we could leave, but we're stuck, just like this one," Luther said, lifting Ginevra's body higher into the air.

"Her name's Ginevra, by the way," Sharur said, hovering back to where the Marquis had first dropped him. "Fine, do what the Marquis asked. Maybe in a thousand years we'll get another opportunity."

"Perhaps. I truly hope so," Luther said, turning toward the exit.

"Luther, before you go, would you like to know the one thing I envy about humans?"

"What's that?"

"They have backbones."

CHAPTER 35
SOL BALAM ARRIVES

Tap . . . tap . . . thump . . . THUMP! THUMP! THUMP!

Edgar hoped that whoever was banging on the front door would just give up, but they kept at it. Could it be the cops? Had one of the neighbors heard all their shouting or maybe even seen what happened?

Edgar's mind raced. What would he say if it was the village police? Gee, I'm sorry, officer, but my mom passed out when she saw the giant praying mantises trying to kidnap my grandfather. What's that? Where's my gramps now? Oh, he's floating above my shoulder. Yeah, like a ghost, but he's just a head. A floating head.

They'd throw him in the loony bin with an explanation like that. Even if he tried sharing his vision with another adult, it might not work. He couldn't risk the possibility.

"Ginevra? Ginevra, are you in there?" The stranger pressed his face against the door's thin side windows. The frosted glass warped and blurred the figure's head, turning it into an inky blob.

"Ginevra!" he croaked, banging on the door now with what sounded like a baton.

"You better get that," Charles said, eyes focused on his unconscious daughter. "Whoever that is, isn't a cop. But if he keeps banging and yelling, they'll be sure to come, and we don't need that kind of attention. Taking care of your mom and finding Aunt Ginnie are our priorities now."

Edgar nodded in agreement and padded to the entrance. As he unbolted the lock, he wondered if he made a fatal mistake. The creatures could be on the other side, pretending to be human, waiting for a moment like this. But nothing came stomping through the unlatched entryway. Instead, an irritated voice asked through the crack, "Oh, for heaven's sake! Is anyone going to let me in?"

Edgar opened the door.

He was surprised that he had to look down to meet the stranger's gaze and even more shocked to see the old man from Aunt Ginnie's photographs. But instead of the desert gear he wore in those snapshots, he stood at the threshold dressed in a sharp, blue three-piece suit. He grasped an elegant black cane topped with a golden monkey head in one hand and a leather briefcase in the other.

What was his name? Samuel, was it? He was definitely a professor. Aunt Ginnie had mentioned the man's name, but Edgar couldn't remember.

"Young man, are we going to stare at each other all day long, or are you going to invite me in?" he asked, raising a bushy eyebrow over his gold-rimmed sunglasses. Edgar caught a glimpse of his own confused reflection in the beetle-black lenses perched on the man's hawkish nose.

"I'm sorry. Who are you?" Edgar asked, rubbing the back of his neck.

"Professor Sol Balam," he said, dropping the briefcase and extending his hand. The brass bracelets on his wrists jingled with the motion. "You must be Edgar Tooms."

Edgar stared at the man's small but muscular hand. Thin silver rings were stacked on each finger up to the knuckle. The image of an owl flashed in his mind. He shook the thought away and clasped Sol's hand.

"It's, um, nice to meet you," Edgar said, stepping aside to let Sol through. "Wait, how'd you get here so soon? Aunt Ginnie said you lived in Connecticut, and she just called you . . ."

"Edgar's right. Even if you were in Greenwich, it would've taken you at least half an hour to get here without traffic," Clara said, intercepting Sol at the living room's threshold.

"You're right, young lady. But I happened to be on the road when Ginevra called, just on the border between New York and Connecticut," Sol said. "And you must be Clara, Ginevra's niece. She's always talking about you."

Clara smiled and let Sol pass. He stopped at the living room's entrance and pointed at Margaret's unconscious body with the tip of his cane. "My goodness, who is this? Why is there an unconscious woman on the living room floor? Is she well?"

"That's my mom," Edgar said. "She passed out when I showed her the Striders."

Sol spun around.

Edgar sucked in a breath. *That was a mistake,* he thought.

Clara smacked her forehead with a palm and pulled Edgar aside. "What are you doing? He's going to think you're crazy!"

"But your aunt told him exactly what she saw. She must trust him. Maybe we should too?"

Sol tapped the cane on the floor, grabbing Edgar and Clara's attention.

"So, Edgar. You shared your vision?" Sol asked, peeking over his sunglasses, giving the children a glimpse of his yellow eyes.

"Yeah. All I have to do is hold someone's hand, like this . . ." Edgar said, stretching out his palm. Sol recoiled and held out his walking stick.

Had he offended the professor? Why did it feel like he was seconds away from another fight? Luckily, Clara stepped between the two of them.

"It's ok. Edgar did it for me, and now I can see them too," she said, holding out her palms.

Sol lowered his cane and stepped close to Clara. His handlebar mustache twitched as he glared at her outstretched hands.

"I'm sorry, I didn't mean to react that way," Sol said, bowing.

"It's ok, but you believe us, right?" Clara asked.

"Yes, yes, I do. Ginevra's voicemail said she saw a Strider," Sol said. "Edgar must have shared his sight with her too."

"Yeah, we all have it now," Edgar said, glancing at Clara. "Two of those giant mantises were just here. They're after my—"

"Grandfather," Sol said, pointing at Opa Chuck who had been, up to that moment, circling Margaret in a loose figure eight pattern.

Charles's mouth dropped open. "You can see me?" he said, floating toward Sol.

"Yes, Mr. Tooms. I can see you."

"H-how?"

"Well, I'm a bit like your grandson here, touched by a type of vision that's very rare in this world." Sol walked around the living room. "I've been able to see and talk to ghosts from a very early age. I've even seen the monsters that are chasing you."

"This is amazing! You're a Seer too!" Edgar said.

Sol shrugged his shoulders.

"So you know what's going on, right? What we're dealing with?" Charles asked.

"Yes, of course." Sol cleared his throat. "Demons of the worst kind."

"How do we keep them away from my grandfather?" Edgar asked.

Sol sighed. "You can't, not for long. If they've set their sights on Charles, they'll keep coming after him—and you too, Edgar."

"Me? Why me?"

"Because you're a Seer, young man. Didn't Ginevra tell you about these special people?"

"Just a bit. Her book said they helped spirits find their way out of the underworld and that they fought the Striders," Edgar replied.

"So you know a little bit about what you're dealing with," Sol said, stepping over Margaret and taking a seat on the couch. He ran a palm over his wedged beard. "Yes, the Seers were great warriors, but they died off. There hasn't been someone like you in this world for thousands of years."

"What about you? You're one too," Clara said.

"Yes, but unlike Edgar here, I've never fought a

Strider."

"But you said that you've seen them."

Sol nodded and balled up his fists.

"But on the rare occasions that I've come across one, I always pretended not to see them. I just . . . turned away out of fear. Have you seen what they do to ghosts?"

Edgar, Charles, and Clara shook their heads.

"It's awful. God-awful. Spirits don't stand a chance against their powers."

"You could've fought them like we did," Edgar said.

"Look at me. I was this small when I was young," Sol said, swinging his legs above the floor. "Don't you think I wanted to? I didn't understand what I was seeing, and I had no idea what I could do back then. But I learned."

"With Aunt Ginnie's book?" Clara asked.

"Correct! Saltus's work filled in the gaps of my knowledge. This is how I know why these creatures see you as a threat. Honestly, I wouldn't be surprised if they're already on their way back to kill you."

"Come on, you're talking to little kids here!" Charles glared at Sol. "You're scaring them."

"Well, it's best not to sugarcoat the news, Mr. Tooms."

"It's ok. The professor's right, Opa," Edgar said. "If they're coming, then we'll fight them."

"Forgive me, but you three don't stand a chance," Sol said. "The Striders will get what they want and find a way to kill anyone that gets in their way."

"No, no, we just fought them off! Aunt Ginnie gave us the Ash of Edom," Clara said, spinning Edgar around and pulling a ziplock bag of Ash from his back pocket. "See? I used it against the biggest one and it totally worked. Burned its face and then they both disappeared."

Sol cackled. "Ginevra always wanted to make that recipe. Well, in that case, you three are off to a bloody good start. But you'll need more of the Ash. Maybe Ginevra can make some . . ." Sol scanned the room. "Where is she?"

"She's gone," Clara said.

"What do you mean, gone?"

Edgar and Clara looked at each other and launched into a high-speed retelling of the Phantid fight. Reaching the end of the tale, Clara knelt beside the black oval singed on the carpet.

"This is the spot where my aunt got sucked up by the Strider's cloud," Clara said, tears welling in her eyes. "She just disappeared. Do you know where she went?"

"Oh, this is bad. This is very, very bad." Sol ran his palms over his shaved head, pacing the room. "Your aunt's been transported to Irkalla, the Strider capital city."

"Irkalla? Where's that?"

"She's in the underworld, my dear."

"I don't understand." Clara shook her head. "Is she dead? Will she be ok?"

"Well, if what the tablets say about this sort of thing is true, then she's not dead, and she can't be killed while she's down there."

"Can we get her back?" Charles asked.

"I'm afraid not. I don't know how to get us down there," Sol said, staring at Opa Chuck bobbing to his right. "You need someone in Irkalla to get her out, but there isn't a Strider there who would betray the Rookery."

"What's the Rookery?" Edgar asked.

Sol exhaled and laced his fingers behind his head. "That's an excellent question. Let's start with what the Rookery was."

CHAPTER 36
HISTORY LESSON

Edgar strained to keep his eyes open.

Sol droned on and on about the Rookery, and as he put it, *its rich, eons-long history*. At first, he paid close attention, especially to the parts about Isimud, the Strider usurper who started a Phantid civil war thousands of years ago and banished the Myrmidons, a race of giant ants and their king, Lugal.

But then, Edgar lost interest when the professor listed off the different species of ghost insects that lived in the Rookery—Myrmidons, Striders, Arachnidae, Termitoidae, and dozens of other hard to pronounce names.

If this was a preview of what a college lecture was like, Edgar wanted no part of it. Just as he was about to doze off, Clara jabbed him in the ribs.

"Listen to this part," she whispered.

Edgar rubbed his eyes and focused his attention on Sol as he paced the room, rubbing his beard.

"There's a strict caste system in place down there," Sol said. "At the very top is the Marquis who rules over the

Rookery, Irkalla, and all the Striders that live in the under-world. Phantids with six or more legs sit on the bottom rungs of this social structure, and at the very bottom are the Phantid slaves, like the termites that built the Rookery."

"How do you know about all this stuff?" Edgar asked.

"Didn't Ginevra read from her copy of *The Forgotten Gods of the Ancient Akkadian Empire*?"

Edgar and Clara nodded.

"Well, then. Saltus actually discovered twenty clay tablets, not just three. Those slabs of clay not mentioned in the book are filled with an almost complete history of Phantids and their world. They're part of my, um, special collection."

"What, you stole them?" Clara asked.

"No, my dear. I won them fair and square. Francis was a bit of a gambler, back in the day, as you kids would say, and I was the better snooker player."

Clara narrowed her eyes. "Wait, how old are you?"

"Very old. Very, very old. Now, that doesn't matter," Sol said, scooting off the couch. "What we should be focused on is getting your aunt back. As I said, there isn't a Strider in the Rookery that would—"

Sol stopped talking and dropped to his haunches and rubbed his beard.

What the hell? Clara mouthed.

Edgar shrugged and walked over to Sol.

"Professor? What's wrong? Why'd you stop?" Edgar asked.

"Not a Strider . . . you'd need a different type of crea-ture, desperate enough to betray the Marquis," Sol said, rising and frantically patting his pockets. "I have to make a call!"

"You can use my cell," Edgar said, offering his thin phone.

"That's kind of you, but I'll be needing something more old-fashioned for this," Sol said, walking toward the kitchen. He stared out the rectangular window above the sink that faced the backyard. Edgar followed Sol's gaze. His eyes seemed focused on a simple red garden shed in the far corner that looked like a miniature barn.

"Edgar, does your mother like to garden?" he asked.

CHAPTER 37
BURROWING

Edgar opened the garden shed's creaky double wooden doors and coughed as dust, desiccated cicada husks, and strands of cobwebs fluttered down. His eyes adjusted to the darkness and focused on a workbench and the white pegboard that hung over it at the far end of the shed.

Tools hung from metal hooks—hammers, trowels, an almost toothless saw, hedge clippers—and sitting atop the wooden workbench was the one piece of machinery his mother forbade him from ever using—an old pneumatic nail gun.

It was his father's and could shoot three-inch nails into solid concrete all day long. Edgar resisted the urge to pick up the bulky tool and focused on finding the posthole digger Sol had asked for.

After a few minutes of sifting through the shed, the best he could find was an old, rusty shovel. He walked out and marched to the center of the yard.

"Will this work?" Edgar asked, angling the blade above his head to block the noonday sun.

"That'll have to do," Sol said, rolling up his sleeves. His suit jacket hung on the lowest branch of the crab apple tree he was standing under. "Give it here, my boy."

Edgar handed the shovel over and watched as Sol sunk the blade into the ground over and over again, scooping out mounds of earth. He was surprised at how strong the professor was for his age. He was a short—under five feet—skinny man, but the sinewy muscles in his arms looked like they belonged to a twenty-year-old.

"Professor, what exactly are you doing?" Edgar asked, sitting on his haunches.

"Burrowing," Sol grunted. "It's how I'll call my friend in the Rookery. Now, no more questions. I need to concentrate."

Edgar rolled his eyes and walked over to Clara who was standing nearby.

"Maybe you were right. Maybe we shouldn't have trusted him. He's acting crazy," Edgar said.

"I don't know. We don't have much choice at this point. Besides, he knows an awful lot about these things. Maybe he's not crazy," Clara said, gazing up at Charles who hovered above them. "What do you think, Opa Chuck?"

"This is all nuts," he said, floating down.

"You three know that I can hear everything, right?" Sol said from the pit he created while the three of them talked.

"Sorry!" Edgar said.

"Now, I need absolute quiet for this next step," Sol said.

"Wait, how'd you dig so fast?" Clara asked.

"Quiet!" Sol yelled.

All Edgar could see of the professor was a glistening,

bald head and the top half of his sunglasses before he dipped out of view.

"What do you think he's doing now?" Edgar asked.

Clara shushed him. "I can hear something. It's like he's mumbling to himself."

"I hear it too," Charles said.

Edgar strained to hear anything beyond the birds chirping or the traffic rolling down the street, but then he heard Sol's voice rising from the hole—the professor was singing!

"What the heck?" Edgar whispered.

"He's chanting. And whatever he's saying, it's not in English," Charles said.

"Akkadian. Definitely Akkadian." Clara smiled.

Edgar and Charles turned to face her.

"What? I'm sure it's Akkadian," Clara said. "Remember my aunt's book? *The Lost Gods of the Akkadian Empire*? He's probably singing something from that."

Edgar shrugged his shoulders. *She's probably right*, he thought. As Sol continued his wailing, Edgar glanced back at the house and wondered if his mom was ok. Clara followed his gaze.

"I'm sure she's fine." She rested a hand on his shoulder. "We checked before coming out here. She's out cold and breathing. Seeing those things was a lot to process."

"Clara's right. Your mom got an eyeful—giant mantises and her dad's floating head," Charles said.

Sol called out. Edgar couldn't understand the words, but it sounded urgent. Edgar peered into the hole and found Sol shaking his head.

"Professor? Are you ok?" Edgar asked, squatting. He

extended his hand, but Sol didn't reach out. Instead, his head shook faster.

"Is he ok?" Clara asked, peering over.

"I don't know. Oh, man! I don't know!" Edgar said.

CHAPTER 38
LONG DISTANCE REUNION

Luther didn't envy the human clasped within his claws. She faced a lifetime of torment behind iron bars. Very few of the living had made their way to Irkalla, and the ones that did ended up as slaves cleaning mushroom gills at the fungal farms or as oddities in the zoo where Ginevra was headed.

But what could he do? Certainly not what Sharur asked of him. Backbones! That snide comment stung Luther deeper than the mace could ever know. The anger grew as he raced through the Rookery's corridors. As he picked up speed, his segmented legs turned into a blur of scuttling blue and Ginevra's hair flowed like a torch.

Luther perseverated on the conversation and a red glow flashed through his body, turning his exoskeleton a deep purple. Striders walking in the opposite direction noticed his vivid color display and jumped out of the way.

Let it go, he told himself, slowing down and unclenching his claws.

He didn't want to hurt Ginevra. None of this was her

fault. He looked down at her and wondered if he was making the right choice. He arched his stinger forward so the weight of the bulbous tip propelled him onward.

Just as he reached the path leading to the zoo, a sharp pain wormed its way through his twelve eyes. The world blurred and the muscles in his claws slackened; Ginevra rolled out of his limp grip and landed with a whimper.

Luther's body curled inward, his claws and legs writhing uncontrollably. A few Striders stopped to watch before quickly moving on, uninterested in the blue scorpion's agony.

Then he heard a voice in his head: *Luther? Luther, can you hear me?*

The words fell like dappled sunlight upon the surface of his tortured nervous system. Slowly, the pain eased and vanished completely.

You? It can't be. It's been so long, Luther said without moving his mouths. Then he felt the presence of a familiar mind settle within his own consciousness. *Ugallu, why are you calling me like this? You know what'll happen to me if we're caught.*

I am sorry, but I had no choice but to burrow. I go by Sol Balam these days, but that's not important. I found a Seer here in Eperu.

Ah, would that be Edgar Tooms? Luther asked, unfurling himself. He picked up Ginevra's body and crawled into an empty passageway as Sol continued talking.

Then there's no doubt that the Marquis is aware of the boy.

He sent General Cressida and her Shadow Striders. Malva's on her way with Andrés too. That child is too much of a threat to be left alive.

That's not good, not good at all.

Even though he was alone with Sol in his head and out of sight, Luther continued to sneak looks at the entryway. His mind wandered and Sol nudged him back into the conversation with a question.

Luther, did you hear me? Sol asked. *A human female should have arrived there recently. Is she there?*

Ginevra?

Yes! How is she?

Unconscious and unharmed, Luther said, setting her down. *But you know how these creatures get when they come down here. It's not natural. The quicker she gets back to her world, the better.*

Good, good. I couldn't bear losing her. Luther, can you get her back?

You too, Ugallu? Luther asked, exhaling audibly.

What? Sol snapped.

Sharur already asked me to bring her over, but I refused.

Good Gods, why?

The Marquis ordered me to take her to the zoo. If I don't, or if she escapes, he'll kill me. Besides, what kind of life could I possibly have up there? I'd grow tired of hiding. I'm not like you, Ugallu.

Luther waited for his friend to reply, but there was a long pause.

Finally, Sol answered, *I'll give you my last travel tablet.*

You would do that? For her? For me? Luther asked, eyes jiggling with excitement.

Yes. It would be worth it.

I'd have to get Sharur to help me.

Good, we can use his strength and speed. When can the three of you get here?

I don't know. The Marquis is in the brothels. We'd have to leave now. But Sol, what could the three of us do against—

"¡Maldito demonio!" someone yelled.

Luther raised his tail, but before he could whip the stinger at the voice, a giant fist punched the underside of his mouth. The strike, from the transformed human, severed the mind link with Sol and hurtled Luther against the corridor's wall.

He turned and watched as the blurry figure slowly stood upon two thin legs; a seam of cold fear squirmed down Luther's armor-plated back. The human was awake.

CHAPTER 39
GINNIE FIGHTS BACK

Luther focused on the human female in front of him. She was even more hideous standing than laying down.

Her enormous, round head stood balanced on a thin neck and the plump hands lolling by her flanks resembled small boulders. One of those had almost knocked him unconscious and was now primed to do worse.

Without thinking, he raised his pincers and flared them open. Ginevra stepped back and raised her fists in response.

"Ginevra? That's your name, right?" Luther asked. "My name is Luther. Now, I want you to stay calm. Please let me explain what's happening."

Luther quickly outlined Ginevra's precarious situation in Irkalla, but the more he spoke, the more agitated she became. He realized that the sight of his insect mouth gesticulating was disturbing for a human. Instead of mandibles, Luther had two glossy, miniature pincers that pawed at the air.

She probably thinks I want to eat her, he thought.

"Ok, listen. I'm going to Su'en. I'm going to change my face. It'll be . . . you know what? It's better if I just show you," Luther said, pointing to his jaw with the tip of his right claw.

There was an audible click as Luther's mouth parts spread apart. Webs of spit crisscrossed the unfurling segments and pattered to the floor. A black vapor followed, pooling around the edges of the growing hole where his jaw used to be.

"Don't be afraid," Luther said, as his human mouth pushed through the mist.

Ginevra retched. Her vomit mixed with Luther's viscous spit on the floor.

"Was that necessary?" Luther's human lips frowned. "I've been told I have a kind-looking pānu."

"What the hell is a pānu?" she asked, wiping spittle from her lips.

"A face, of course," Luther said, as the black mist cleared around his flat nose and round chin.

"You remind me of those giant stone Olmec heads. Well, half of one."

"I'll take that as a compliment."

"You're a Phantid, aren't you?"

"Yes. How did you know that?"

"I studied some of your history. Sol insisted that your kind were real. I never thought that I'd actually—"

"I was just talking to Sol," Luther said, clicking his claws.

"My Sol? Sol Balam?"

"Yes. As I said, I was just talking to him, but you—"

"How is that possible? How could he just be talking with you?"

"You know, this would go a lot faster if you'd stop interrupting me. Sol's convinced me to help you get out of here. Now, are you going to listen to my plan?"

Ginnie raised her hand.

"Oh, my Gods. What?"

"Why do you have a pānu?"

"It's what your scientists would call an adaptation," Luther said, smiling. "Now, let me tell you about my plan."

CHAPTER 40
BAD NEWS FIRST

Edgar didn't understand how Sol's head was still attached to his neck. It shook side to side so fast that it resembled a pink, oblong blur. A long moan escaped his mouth as his lips and cheeks flapped. The furious motion sent motes of dirt flying from the hole the professor stood in.

Then Sol stopped moving.

Clara squeezed Edgar's shoulder. "Why does his face look so . . . surprised?"

"I don't know." Edgar knelt and leaned closer to the hole. "Maybe he had a heart—"

Sol arched his head back and sucked in a long breath of air. A plume of dust erupted from his mouth, and he turned in place and picked up his sunglasses.

"I'm sorry, you two. I didn't mean to scare you. My call was interrupted, and it's taken me a bit to recover," he explained, crawling out from the hole. He stood, patted the dust off his ruined suit, and cleared his throat.

"What happened?" Edgar asked. "Did the call work?"

"Oh, yes, it did," Sol said, wiping his cheek with the

back of his hand. He flicked away a glob of mud. "Now, do you want the bad news or the good news?"

Edgar considered the question. "The bad."

"You know, Edgar. I think you and I are going to get along just fine," Sol said, smiling. "The Rookery's sending assassins to kill everyone in this house."

"Jesus Christ. This is awful," Charles said, shaking his head. The motion sent him twisting up into the air and back down again. "This is my fault. These things wouldn't have come if I wasn't around."

"Opa! Calm down. It's going to be ok." Edgar reached for his grandfather with outstretched palms, but Opa Chuck darted upward.

"Edgar's right. It's going to be okay, and this isn't your fault," Clara said.

"You've seen those things. Your aunt's gone, and I can't do anything to help." Charles spiraled toward the grass. Opa Chuck bounced and then sunk halfway into the earth.

"Get a grip, sir!" Sol snapped. He dropped to his haunches and ripped off his sunglasses. He glared at Charles. "Look at my eyes, Mr. Tooms. I'm not going to let them take you or your grandson. Do we understand each other?"

Charles blinked and slowly rose.

"I'm sorry," Charles said, inhaling deeply. "I didn't mean to lose it."

"No need to apologize." Sol stood, hooking his sunglasses on his ears. "Now, does everyone want to hear the good news?"

"Yes, please!" Edgar said.

"Ginevra is on her way back."

"Yes!" Clara cheered. "When's she getting here?"

"I'm not sure, but she'll be coming back with my friend Luther and a special weapon called Sharur."

"What's a Sharur?" Edgar asked.

"An enchanted mace, of course." Sol cracked his knuckles.

"Will that help us fight off the Striders?" Clara asked.

"Oh, yes. Sharur is a powerful weapon, but if they don't get here soon, then we have to fend for ourselves with whatever we have." Sol placed a hand on Clara's shoulder. "My dear, do you know where your aunt keeps her skeletons?"

Clara nodded. "Yeah, she's got loads of bones left at—"

"Oh, Lord!" Opa said.

Edgar turned and followed his grandfather's gaze toward the house. A figure moved in the kitchen, its features blurred by the sun's gleaming reflection.

"Is . . . is that Mom?"

Sol nodded. "It appears to be."

Edgar shielded his eyes. The professor was right. His mother was staring at them, hands covering her mouth. She looked scared.

"Don't worry, Edgar. I'll go talk to her," Opa said, puttering forward.

"Absolutely not!" Sol raised a hand. "Can you imagine what seeing your floating decapitated head would do to your daughter right now?"

"She's my daughter and she deserves to know that truth about what's happening. Besides, I think she can already see me and—"

"And just look at the state of her!" Sol pointed a finger toward Margaret. Edgar could see tears running down her cheeks.

"Opa, Sol's right," Edgar said. "Mom's terrified. She doesn't understand what's happening."

"Let's take this slow," Sol said. "Why don't you let me and Edgar talk to her first? Your grandson will calm her down and I can explain everything that's happening."

Opa nodded. "Fine, you two go."

CHAPTER 41
MESMERISM

Edgar stopped at the kitchen threshold. His mother stood at the sink, staring out the window. She held a rolling pin in one hand and tapped it against her thigh.

She's freaked out, Edgar thought. Who could blame her? She just saw two giant praying mantises and a floating, talking head—her father's. At least Edgar grew up with the sight of Opa's ghostly noggin. Ghosts, at least Opa's, were normal for him.

Aunt Ginnie had handled her new powers well, but she seemed prepared, eager even, to see through Edgar's eyes. But Mom didn't even get a warning, and now she seemed on the verge of a breakdown.

"Mom? Are you ok?"

"Edgar, honey. What the hell is going on? Why does that balloon . . ." She jutted her chin toward the yard. ". . . have a face?"

Edgar puffed air out from his cheeks. He glanced at Sol who put a reassuring palm on his shoulder.

"Tell her the truth," he whispered.

"It's not a balloon, Mom. That's Opa Chuck."

"No!" Margaret slammed the rolling pin onto the wooden countertop. "Your grandfather's dead!" She slammed the pin again. "You can't see him! I didn't see him . . . I don't want to see him."

"Your son's telling the truth, Mrs. Tooms," Sol said. "That's your father out there."

Margaret turned and pointed the pin at the professor. "Who the hell are you?"

"I'm professor Sol Balam and I'm glad to see that you're awake."

Margaret blushed.

"Oh, don't be embarrassed. You witnessed something extraordinarily disturbing. Most people would pass out at the sight of them. They're frightening, aren't they?" Sol asked, placing two wriggling forefingers above his forehead. "The mantises?"

Margaret dropped the rolling pin. "Christ. I didn't imagine them, did I?"

"No, Mom. You didn't. They're real and—"

Margaret scooped Edgar into her arms. "Honey, I am so sorry—so sorry—that I never believed you. I am so ashamed of myself for hitting you."

Was this really happening? Did she finally believe him? Edgar squeezed back. "It's ok, Mom. It's ok."

"No, no. I had no right to raise my hand," she said, pushing Edgar back slightly. She looked into his eyes and frowned. "Can you forgive me?"

"Yeah, Mom. I forgive you," he said, nodding. He hugged her again. "I forgive you."

Sol coughed. Margaret snapped her head toward the professor.

"As I was saying, Striders are a species of demon from the underworld."

"And they're coming back, Mom," Edgar said. "Sol's been talking to his friend in the Rookery, and he has a plan to—"

"Rookery?" Margaret shook her head. "What in the world is a Rookery?"

"Mrs. Tooms, I know this is a lot to take in, but you and your family are in terrible danger. The mantises you saw earlier are nothing compared to the Shadow Striders heading up here now."

"More? More of those things are coming? Can't we call the police?"

"No, the police can't help us."

Margaret turned and pulled a long carving knife from a woodblock on the counter. "Then we fight, right?" She waved the blade in the air. "They're just bugs. Big, ugly—"

Sol clapped his hands together so hard that Edgar covered his ears and Margaret froze in place. The professor reached into his suit pocket and pulled out a metal lighter.

"Listen to my voice, Mrs. Tooms." Sol flicked open the silver-plated Zippo. A sharp yellow flame licked the air. "Put away all fear and pay attention."

Margaret's eyes fluttered closed, her arms dropped to the side, and her head lolled from side to side. She groaned and the knife slipped from her hands and its tip pierced the linoleum.

"You're going to accept the fact that ghosts are real, that demons are real, and that your father exists as a spirit in this world—"

"Sol! What are you doing?" Edgar asked.

"Moving things along with some mesmerism."

"Mesmerism? Is that like hypnosis?"

Sol nodded.

"Why do you need to do that?"

"I don't think your mother can handle the truth without some help. It might drive her insane. Do you want to risk that?"

Edgar shook his head.

"Good. Now let me work." Sol turned his attention toward Margaret. "Mrs. Tooms, when I extinguish this flame, we're all going outside to talk about how we're going to protect your family. Do you understand?"

Margaret nodded.

The lighter snapped shut and Margaret's eyes opened.

"What happened?" she asked.

"I was just asking if you had any weapons, other than knives, in the house? We need to start preparing for the invasion," Sol said.

For the briefest of moments, Edgar had forgotten about the Strider threat.

"We don't have any guns, professor," Edgar said.

"Technically, we do," Margaret said.

Edgar's eyes widened.

"Your dad's old nail gun. It's in the garden shed."

"That's better than nothing." Sol turned to Margaret. "Why don't we go out and get what we need while you have a chat with your father. I'm sure he wants to say hello."

Margaret turned toward the window and bit her nails. "Sure. I can do that."

Edgar shook his head. He couldn't believe what was

happening. Mom was about to see and talk to Opa at the same time.

"Not bad, huh?" Sol asked.

"How long's the hypnosis last?"

Sol shrugged his shoulders. "We'll see."

CHAPTER 42

ONBOARDING MARGARET

Edgar patted the gray nail gun cradled in his arms and grinned. A long, coiled yellow tube trailed behind him as he marched toward the center of the backyard. Behind him, Sol grunted as he dragged a squat air compressor out from the garden shed. The machine's metal feet carved deep, moist furrows in the grass.

"I can help with that," Edgar said, glancing backward. Sol shouted a warning, but it was too late. The nail gun's yellow tubing wrapped around Edgar's ankles like tentacles, sending him tumbling into the grass. The nail gun escaped his grip and slid on the grass.

A few feet away, he could see his mom and Opa talking. He still couldn't believe his eyes. The spell Sol put on his mom seemed to be working. She patched up whatever differences she had with Opa during their tear-filled reunion. But now they turned and scowled in Edgar's direction.

"Professor! I thought you were going to handle this?

I've told my son a thousand times this machine's off limits," Margaret said, crossing her arms.

"Your mom's right. That's a SENCO SN60—it can drive a three-inch nail through a pair of stacked two-by-fours," Opa Chuck added. "It's way too dangerous for you to be playing with."

"Thank you," Margaret said, nodding sharply at Opa.

Edgar frowned. He had dreamed of this day for years, but never expected the two of them to team up and scold him. That was a bummer.

"Mom, the compressor's too heavy for me to budge. Besides, the nailer's not loaded and I can't shoot it without power." Edgar jingled the yellow hose in his hand. "And you have to connect this tube from the handle into the compressor."

"Edgar's right, ma'am. It's perfectly safe for him to be carrying it," Sol said.

"I'll say when it's safe!" Margaret said.

As his mom and the professor argued, Clara pulled Edgar aside.

"How is your mom acting so cool with all this? It's weird."

"Sol hypnotized her."

Clara's eyes widened. "Get out!"

"Yeah, he made so she'd just go with the flow," Edgar said.

"That's wild. Wait!"

"Do you think Sol put a spell on us?"

Edgar shook his head. When would he have had the time? He saw how he did it and—

Margaret clapped her hands together. "Alright, everyone. The professor here is going to go over how we're going to fight these things."

Sol wiped the mud from his trousers. "No, Mrs. Tooms, we're not going on the offensive. We're making our stand here—in your house."

Margaret laughed. "What, like the Alamo? Don't you teach history, professor? Don't you remember what happened to the defenders?"

"Well, we're not going to suffer the same fate. Now, do you want to hear my plan, or not?"

Margaret rolled her eyes. "And how exactly are we going to make our stand?"

"To start, we're going to make more Ash of Edom," Sol said.

Edgar noticed his mother's baffled stare and tugged at her arm. "The bug powder we used earlier in the house. Remember?"

Margaret nodded.

"Yes, the bug powder as you call it. It's a potent weapon that can kill these creatures. I'll need Clara to get whatever bones Ginevra has left at her house," Sol said. "We'll mix anything leftover with water and make a paste to coat the tips of nails and spears—"

"Spears? What are you talking about? We don't have any spears in the house," Margaret said. She waved her arms in front of Sol's face. "Hello? Professor?"

Sol rubbed his beard and paced. "We'll also need balloons. Lots of balloons."

"Are we throwing a shindig for these things, professor?" Charles asked, raising an eyebrow.

"Yes, a surprise party for the surprise party." Sol chuckled.

"Hello? Why isn't anyone listening to me?" Margaret asked.

"I'm sorry, Mrs. Tooms. It's just that there isn't much we can use as weapons, and I'm trying to work with what we have. Speaking of, would you happen to have any barley flour in the kitchen?"

"Barley flour?" Margaret rubbed her eyes with the heel of her palms and groaned. This is it, Edgar thought. This is the moment Sol's spell breaks and Mom loses her cool.

"Actually, yes. We have some," Margaret said, placing a hand on her hip. "I don't understand how baking's going to help us."

"It's not, but we are going to cook up some magic in your kitchen," Sol said.

CHAPTER 43
BROKEN PLANS

Sol rubbed the scar on the underside of his chin—a gift from a German soldier given a lifetime ago. Back then, the professor held off a platoon of Nazis with a half-spent handgun, a smoke grenade, and a rusty shovel, saving his regiment.

Today, he would have given his right arm for those meager supplies. The makeshift weapons assembled on the kitchen counter resembled a pathetic flea market stall: piles of black balloons, sharpened broom sticks, half-used bags of flour, Pyrex mixing bowls filled with the Ash of Edom, and one pneumatic nail gun.

He dipped his hand into the Ash and sifted through the coarse salt and bone fragments with his fingertips. Clara had brought a sack full of bones from her aunt's curio and did a beautiful job of grinding and mixing the ossified remains into three bowls of the deadly powder.

Despite the quality of Clara's work, he knew it wouldn't be enough. Like he told Edgar and his family, they couldn't go on the offensive. Not with these limited tools. The only bright spot was the nail gun, but there was no way to know if Ash-coated nails would even work against the Striders. Still, they'd have to try.

Margaret picked up a paper sack of barley flour. "I still don't understand what this is for."

Sol arched an eyebrow. He'd forgotten that he'd only given the group the broad strokes of his plan. "We're going to use the flour to draw Zisurrûs."

"Scissor-roos? I'm sorry, what are Scissor-roos?" Margaret asked.

"It's pronounced . . . you know what? It doesn't matter," Sol said, throwing his hands up. He raised his voice. "All you need to know is that I'll draw a few magical circles with the flour in the front yard, basement, and attic to prevent Striders from transporting. That's going to force them through a choke point in the backyard so we can attack them on our terms."

"Here's the water you asked for," Edgar said, setting a gurgling pitcher and a small plastic bucket on the table. "Want me to get started?"

Sol smiled. "Yes, scoop a few cups of the Ash into the bucket and mix it with a wee bit of water until it's a thick paste. Like pancake batter." Sol leaned on the edge of the table. "We'll coat the nails and broomstick spears with it. That's going to help us pierce through a Strider's thick armor."

"You don't sound confident about that," Charles said, furrowing his brow. "Ash-filled balloons, broomstick spears, choke points? Is any of this really going to work? Margaret and I don't have combat experience. Hell, I don't even have hands! And Edgar and Clara are just kids."

"It could . . . it should," Sol muttered. He met Charles's

gaze and exhaled. "You're right, Mr. Tooms. This isn't going to work. Without Luther and Sharur here, I'm afraid we don't stand a chance. We need more help."

"Couldn't you make another call? Like you did with Luther and get some more friends to come over?" Clara asked.

"I wish I could, but I don't know anyone else in the Rookery." Sol watched Edgar as he mixed the paste. The boy was lost in the chore as everyone around him talked. It was a simple and mind-numbing task. Mesmerizing, really. Sol stared at the miniature whirlpool Edgar created as he swirled the wooden spoon around the bright orange plastic container. Round and round. Down and down.

The motion ignited an idea in Sol's mind.

CHAPTER 44

THE NECRONAUT

"Clara, you're a genius!" Sol danced around the table. "We might have some friends!"

"Who?" Clara asked.

"The Myrmidon!" Sol grasped Clara's hands.

"The ants Isimud banished?" Clara said, hopping in a circle with Sol.

"That's right," Sol said, smiling. "You're a future professor, like your aunt, my dear!"

"You think they'll help us?" Edgar asked.

"Oh, yes, they'll jump at this opportunity." Sol paused his dance with Clara. "They've been sweltering in the underworld for thousands of years."

"Will you need the shovel again?" Edgar asked, scraping the side of the bucket with the spoon.

"No, m'boy. This requires a face-to-face meeting with Lugal, king of the ants. And you're the one who has to go down to Kur."

Edgar stopped stirring. "Wait, what? Why?"

"Only a young Seer like you can make it down to Kur.

I'm too old. The trip'll tear me apart. It won't be easy on you either—"

"Whoa, whoa, whoa. Wait right there! There's no way you're sending my son down to, wherever it is you said," Margaret stammered.

"Kur, the underworld beneath the underworld," Sol said.

"Oh! Is that it? The underworld beneath the underworld," Charles said, rolling his eyes. "Lord, that sounds dangerous."

Sol nodded. "Yes, it's a potentially deadly trip, but if we don't get help soon, we're guaranteed to die by the sharp end of a Strider's claw."

"Why's the trip so dangerous?" Edgar asked.

Sol met Edgar's gaze. The boy deserved to know. But how much should he tell him? Too much detail and he'd refuse. Or his mother might put her foot down, rightfully so. Not enough detail and the boy'll never forgive him for what he was about to send him through. The boy seemed determined. He'd give him just enough then.

"Human beings—living human beings—aren't meant to cross into the netherworld. Spirits like your grandfather could potentially do it, but that's because he doesn't have a physical body anymore. You do."

"So?"

"So, we're bending the rules of the universe to get you down there and that means your body's going to go through a very uncomfortable change," Sol explained.

"Like an astronaut then? Their bodies get squished when they take off, right?"

Sol was impressed. The boy's analogy wasn't too far off the mark. "Well, in this case, you'd be a necronaut."

"No! Absolutely not!" Margaret slammed her hands on the table.

"Mom! We don't have a choice," Edgar said. "We're going to need help. These Striders are strong. Stronger than all of us put together."

"Your son is right. We don't stand a chance without the Myrmidon," Sol said, admiring Edgar's determination. He flicked open his lighter and closed it.

"This is insane," Margaret mumbled.

"I think our definition of insane has changed drastically these past couple of days," Charles said. "I think we should consider letting Edgar do it."

"I am doing it. I'm going to Kur," Edgar said, rolling up his sleeves. He looked at Sol and rubbed his arms. "How am I going to do that exactly?"

"I'll show you," Sol said.

He walked out of the dining room and fetched his briefcase and placed the leather case on the table. His nimble fingers toyed with the combination lock. The black numbers on gold wheels blurred with each flick and nudge. As the last digit slid into place, the brass lock opened with a click.

"This, my friends, is a travel tablet," Sol said, opening the case. He pointed at the small rectangle nestled in the case's foam interior and ran a finger over the engraved cuneiform glyphs. "The inscription you see scratched onto the surface is an ancient Akkadian chant that can transport the singer to any of the seven worlds."

"Akkadian?" Edgar asked. "I have to sing that?"

"Just the first three lines and I'll write out the translation phonetically," Sol said, placing a hand on Edgar's shoulder. "It won't take more than thirty minutes to memorize. I promise."

Clara ducked under Sol's arms. "How old is it?"

"This clay tablet dates back to 3,000 BCE," Sol explained, smacking Clara's hand as she reached for the glass vials nestled in the dark cushioning next to the tablet. "We're not touching those just yet."

Edgar chuckled as Clara rubbed her hand.

"Ok, so what do I do next?" Edgar asked.

"You'll need to strip," Sol said.

Clara laughed as Edgar blushed.

CHAPTER 45
GIDDYUP!

Ginnie flattened herself against Luther's back as the scorpion scurried through cramped, ill-lit tunnels. Above, jagged stalactites threatened to shred her back as Luther picked up speed through the narrowing corridors.

She craned her neck backward and breathed a sigh of relief as Sharur rocketed through the caverns just a few feet behind. Chunks of rock and debris pinged off his metallic head.

No need to worry about me, Ginevra. I'm doing fine. It'll take more than a few pebbles to hurt me, the mace said through his mind link.

Ginnie shivered. She didn't like how easily Sharur could read her thoughts or the way he sent his thoughts through the invisible channel between them. Still, it was comforting to know that in this strange world she had two allies willing to risk their lives to save hers.

Sharur had immediately forgiven Luther when he presented his apology and plan for escape back at the Marquis's chamber. The mace added a few suggestions of his own to smooth out the kinks in Luther's idea, and the three were off to the Royal Teleportation Terminal with a simple goal: trick the traffic controller into letting them all travel to Ginnie's world.

"You ok back there?" Luther asked.

"Yeah, of course!" Ginnie yelled.

"Good, because we're almost there!"

Suddenly, the path dropped into a near vertical descent. Ginnie's fingers dug into the fleshy gap between Luther's armored plates and squeezed.

"Ow! Don't pull too hard!" Luther hissed.

"Can't you slow down?" Ginnie pressed her face against Luther's cold outer shell. Her stomach churned with the fall. "Isn't there an easier path?"

"These abandoned tunnels are the quickest way to the teleportation chambers, and they help us avoid running into any curious Striders who might wonder why I'm carrying a living human being on my back." Luther slowed as the path's incline leveled out.

"What's wrong? Why'd we stop?" she asked, as Luther paused in front of a dark wall. "Did we hit a dead end?"

Luther fiddled with a loose stone, pushing it flush against the wall until the sound of enormous metal gears turning and falling into place echoed through the tunnel. A rectangular slab of rock slid inward on unseen hinges, giving Luther and his cargo just enough space to pass.

"We're here," Sharur said, floating next to her and Luther. "Now, remember to play dead. No matter what you hear, don't open your eyes. Once they let us into a teleportation chamber, it'll take seconds to get back to Eperu."

"I remember. You two are going to do all the hard

work. I just lay here," Ginnie said, closing her eyes and letting her body slacken. She patted Luther's shell with her palms and heels. "Giddyup, Luther. Let's do this!"

Luther grumbled. "I'm not a . . . what's it called? A work whore."

Ginnie laughed. "You mean, workhorse?"

"Not that, either."

CHAPTER 46
ESCAPE FROM IRKALLA

Luther crawled halfway out of the secret entrance and stopped. His twelve black eyes twitched and jiggled as they adjusted to the Royal Teleportation Terminal's brightly lit interior.

"Why'd you stop?" Sharur asked from behind. "The door's going to close on us if we don't keep moving."

"It's too bright," Luther hissed, raising his claws to shield the eyes on his head and those studding the outer edges of his face.

"This is taking too long," Sharur said, shoving Luther's rump.

"Hey, there's no need for that," Luther said, but there wasn't much he could do against the staff's strength. Luther's three-pronged feet squealed against the smooth marble floor as he was shoved into the chamber.

Dozens of Striders and pill bugs on leather leashes turned to stare. They quickly lost interest and disappeared into the mass of other Striders making their way through the facility. Sharur slowly slid through the air and righted himself next to Luther as the stones behind them slid back into place with a hiss.

"Have you ever been here before?" Sharur asked.

"Never," Luther said, admiring the vaulted ceiling above their heads. Legions of fireflies skittered across the tiled surface, illuminating the vast chamber with their blazing white rumps.

"It's laid out like an oversized cathedral," Sharur said. "You could stand a thousand Ginevras side by side with their arms outstretched and they'd never touch the walls. This corridor stretches forward twice that length."

"I want to see!" Ginnie whispered, opening her eyes to narrow slits.

"Shhh! Stay absolutely quiet and still," Sharur said. "And close your eyes!"

Luther admired the chamber's walls—millions of glossy, blue bricks bordered alternating bands of gold and amber tiles that shimmered like fish scales.

Enormous alcoves, two stories tall, dotted the facade at regular intervals, breaking up the field of lustrous lapis lazuli with pitch-black entrances that seemed to stretch impossibly deep. Dozens of Striders queued up at each one, waiting for a turn to enter.

"Those are the transportation chambers. Watch how the Striders use them," Sharur said, nodding toward a mantis with a clay tablet perched in its claw tip. "All you have to do is insert a travel tablet into the slot on the side and step through the darkness."

Luther listened, but his eyes were focused on the intricate mosaics set between each archway. Images of Phantids with six or more legs were rare in the Rookery, so it was shocking to see the walls here stamped with tiled collages of arachnids, ants, sprawling millipedes, beetles, and dozens of other creatures designated by four-legged Striders as Crawlers.

Luther scurried toward the artwork.

"Hey, where are you going?" Sharur asked.

"I just want a closer look," Luther said, stopping in front of one of the mosaics.

Ginevra grumbled as the momentum scooted her body against the grain of Luther's armor.

"Just a look . . ." Luther mumbled to Ginevra.

He ran a claw tip over the scratched face of a beetle. He moved to the next portrait and noticed the same damage done to a spider. Only the mosaics featuring mantises were unharmed.

"Bastards," Luther mumbled, scuttling back to Sharur. "They've defaced all of the sections with Crawlers."

"I think that happened back when Isimud took over. Such a shame," Sharur said. "Well, there's nothing we can do about that. Let's concentrate on getting out of here, my friend."

Luther snipped at the air with his claws. "Yes, yes. Where to now?"

"We need a travel tablet," Sharur said, turning to face a large brass booth halfway down the center. "That's the traffic controller's hut. We need to convince the operator there to give us a tablet with the coordinates Malva used on her last trip."

Luther sighed. He wondered if their plan would actually work. They were already drawing too much attention. Striders stared at Ginevra lying flat on his back and pointed claws at Sharur. It was unusual to see the Marquis's staff on its own.

"Don't worry about them," Sharur said, floating ahead.

Luther raced forward as Sharur stopped short and bounced, his solid round pommel echoing against the hard floor.

"Attention! Everyone stand clear, the Marquis's personal secretary is here on royal business!" Sharur parted the crowd of Phantids with his thunderous voice. "Stand aside! Stand aside!"

So much for keeping a low profile, Luther thought. Ginevra's feet clacked against his casing.

"Why's Sharur shouting?" she asked.

"I don't know. He's gone off plan, the crazy staff," Luther whispered, crawling toward the center of the facility.

By the time he reached the booth, a large crowd of Striders had gathered. *This was a mistake*, Luther thought, feeling dozens of green, brown, and purple compound eyes focused on him. He tapped the ornate booth with his pincer and stepped backward.

"Hello? I'm here to take a package to Eperu on behalf of the Marquis," Luther said.

Chittering laughter erupted on all sides.

"Did you hear that? This Crawler thinks he's going to travel!" An emerald-green Strider snorted, unleashing tendrils of black smoke in the air through its human mouth. The pill bug by its legs tumbled onto its segmented back and laughed, clutching its underside with thin, transparent legs.

Sharur rose above the chuckling Strider and glared. "Do you know who I am?" he asked.

The Strider snapped his mouth parts shut and bowed his head. His thin antennae drooped overs his hard snout.

"I see that you do. Good, very good. Then you should also know that if you offend the Marquis's personal secretary, then you offend your Lord as well, yes?"

"I-I'm sorry, Sharur. I meant nothing by it. We don't see too many Crawl—um, I mean scorpions here," he said, scooping up his balled up pill bug pet and patting its shell with the side of its claw. "Please, please don't inform the Marquis."

"You're not worth the effort," Sharur grunted and spun to face the other mantises. Claws tucked inward and wings fluttered shut. "All of you, leave us to our business."

As the Striders retreated, the traffic controller crawled out of the booth, swiveling her blunt brown head left and right to survey the scene. Her quivering green eyes settled on Luther.

"What are you doing here without the Marquis? And what in the worlds is that on your back?" she asked, pointing at Ginevra.

"Operator, what's your name?" Luther countered.

"Lanike."

"Well, Lanike. We're here on royal business," Luther said, shifting his weight to keep Ginevra's body from rolling off. "We're to deliver this human back to her home in Eperu. We'll need the same coordinates Malva used on her last trip."

"There's been no official request. You know that I need the Marquis's say-so for any trip by someone of your, um, class," Lanike said, shaking her head.

"Our Lord sent me—sent us—to do this," Luther hissed, tapping Sharur.

"She doesn't believe you," the staff whispered.

"You're going to ruin this," Luther said, swatting his stiff tail at Sharur's face. Luther turned to Lanike. He unfurled his mouth parts and let his human face smile. "Let me explain why our Lord sent us."

As he laid out his story, Lanike crawled out of the booth and crouched by his side for a closer look at Ginevra. He was about to warn her not to get closer, but Lanike sprang backward before he could say anything.

"Its eyes opened!" she shouted. "Gods! I've never seen a living one up close like this. They're so . . . ugly."

"Yes! So you see why the Marquis wants it out of the Rookery, right? Her presence taints its sanctity. Now, please give me the tablet."

Lanike shook her head up and down and then side to side. Damn! They were so close. More Striders approached the booth, drawn by the spectacle unfolding. Luther opened his mouth to speak but stopped as he heard the Marquis's booming voice behind him.

He turned to see Sharur's painted eyes glow a bright red.

"Do as you're told, or I'll have my niece carve your family open," Sharur said in the Marquis's voice.

"My Lord! I didn't realize your presence was here," Lanike said, rushing back into the booth. Her claws became a blur as she etched coordinates into fresh clay. She handed the tablet down to Luther. "Here, take it! My apologies, eh?"

"Thank you, Lanike," Luther said, snatching the tablet. "Which chamber should we use?"

"Pick whichever you like," said Lanike, pointing to the left. "That one! There's no one waiting there."

Luther chuckled and marched toward the empty chamber.

"This is it," Ginevra said in a low voice, pounding Luther's back with her oversized fist. You said that I'll turn back to normal once we're through. Right?"

"Correct, and we're almost there," Luther said, stopping in front of the entrance. He shuddered. The darkness standing between them and their freedom was an impenetrable wall of shadow. Not even the living light from the ceiling reflected off the void's flat surface.

"Well? Are we going?" Sharur asked.

Luther stepped slightly to the side, glad to turn his gaze away from the nothingness in front of him, and slipped the travel tablet into the slot. Something within the tile work clicked and a subtle flash of light shimmered across the entrance.

"Yes, let's go," Luther said, grasping Sharur in his right claw. The scorpion stepped forward and was sucked into the chamber.

CHAPTER 47

THE CHANT

Edgar stripped down to his underwear and sat cross-legged in the center of the living room. A few inches from his bare feet rested the clay travel tablet and a glass vial. Sol said that these were the only things he needed to travel to Kur. And a singing voice.

"Are you ready?" the professor hollered from the kitchen.

"Sure. I'm half naked for whatever reason you're not telling me. You crazy old man," Edgar muttered.

At the very least, Edgar was able to take his clothes off without Clara watching. Still, she and his mother had to witness Edgar in this state for most of the ceremony. It was embarrassing, but he knew he had to do it.

"Yeah, I'm good. Everyone can come in now," Edgar shouted.

Opa Chuck was the first to zip into the room, followed by Margaret, Clara, and Sol. The professor stepped in front of Edgar and kneeled. He picked up the glass vial and twisted open the metal cap.

"This is the Oil of Uruk," Sol said, muddling the viscous, amber liquid between his palms. He then smeared the oil across Edgar's face, shoulders, chest, and arms.

"Ugh, it smells like that goop Mom rubs on my chest when I'm sick," Edgar said, bringing the back of his palm to his forehead.

Sol smacked his hand away. "Do you know how hard this resin is to come by? Now, do you remember what happens after you arrive in Kur?"

"I wait for Lugal to appear and request his help." Edgar raised an eyebrow. "Will it really be that easy? He's just going to say yes?"

"It's that simple. Besides, the Ant King has to obey a Seer's request," Sol said. "Alright, Edgar. It's time to concentrate on the next step."

Edgar grunted and picked up the brown tablet and held it in his palm. It was about the same size as his mother's new e-book reader and just as thin. His fingers ran across the wedges and circles carved into its surface. The designs looked like an ancient computer code. Luckily, he didn't have to read any of the symbols. All he had to do was sing a simple, three-line chant that Sol taught him.

"Is this going to work?" Charles asked. "Is Edgar really going to travel?"

"Yes, all he has to do is start the song, and I'll pick it up after the first three lines. Your grandson is literally going to vanish for a few moments. So, be prepared for that. All of you," Sol said, glancing around the room.

"Be careful, Edgar," Clara said, smiling.

"I will," Edgar said. "I'm ready."

"Good," Sol said. "Let us begin. Start with the first line, m'boy."

Edgar closed his eyes and inhaled deeply. As he exhaled, the strange melody slithered out of his mouth and hung in the air. That wasn't so hard. The second line came even easier, but then Edgar's mind drew a blank.

He couldn't remember the final words. He groaned and felt sweat bead on his forehead. He was about to open his eyes and apologize for screwing up, but Sol's hand gripped his shoulder before he could speak.

"You're doing fine, m'boy," the professor said, his voice trailing into echo. "Keep singing and keep your eyes closed. You're doing fine."

Was he singing? He couldn't tell anymore. He heard Sol pick up the song. He said they would be singing in Akkadian. The words sounded so strange, so dreamlike. Then silence—he heard nothing but his own breath and heartbeat.

Edgar felt at peace in this newfound stillness. It was as if he was floating in a pool of black water. A sharp pain in his knees quickly ended the reverie. He reached down, but something pulled his arms over his head and straightened his legs. Edgar opened his eyes, but all he could see was black.

He screamed as some unseen force pulled his body in two opposite directions. Before he passed out, he heard his bones pop and snap.

CHAPTER 48
TRAVEL TO KUR

Cold droplets pattered over Edgar's forehead, waking him from a deep slumber. He groaned and focused on the water streaming down the tips of slate gray stalactites hanging high overhead. He raised a hand to block the stream and thrust it back down.

Why was his hand the size of a hubcap?

Edgar rolled over and pushed himself up. He looked down at his squat body, gargantuan hands and feet, and thin, flesh-colored tubes for the arms and legs they were connected to.

"I look like Mickey Mouse," Edgar whispered.

God, if his body looked this bizarre, what did his face look like? He shuddered and raised his hands up, gently patting the outer edges of his lemon-shaped head.

He closed his eyes and ran his plump, sausage fingers down his face. The skin was smooth and tacky to touch. His eyes were bulbous disks, a round nub replaced his nose, and his mouth had shrunk into a tiny, lipless hole.

"W-what's happened to me?" he yelled.

He turned and ran, his giant feet throwing up clouds of dust, but there was nowhere to go. He was stranded in a desolate field of volcanic rock and ash. The air was thick with soot, reverberating with the sound of water dripping.

The flat landscape stretched in all directions, dotted with glossy boulders. Above, a vast cloud of stony fingers. Thick veins of crimson light rippled between the stalactites, casting a bloody glow over the gray world.

"Sol! Professor? Can you hear me?" Edgar shouted, picking up the pace. The tuft of blond hair on his head swept back like a match in the wind. "There's nothing here. I don't see the Ant King!"

Thump!

Edgar slammed into a boulder. He turned just in time to see the rock tremble. It wasn't a rock—it was the butt end of a gigantic ant. The creature reared to an almost standing position. Its egg-shaped bottom crunched against the rocky soil as its stiff legs splayed out and anchored the burgundy creature in place.

"Oh, god. I'm sorry!" Edgar said, curling into a ball.

The ant turned its square, eyeless head skyward and roared. Flecks of green spittle sprayed from between its horn-like mandibles. A bit of the goo landed near Edgar's feet and sizzled.

"Stay absolutely still," a voice warned. "My soldier ants are practically blind, but they'll march toward any movement, however slight, and attack."

Edgar did as he was told and froze in place. He felt the ground around him shift as another ant crawled closer. Its thick antennae, bristling with brown hairs, came into view.

Their rounded ends tickled Edgar's body and whipped away.

"As I suspected, a human boy. A live one too," the voice said, twitching its antennae.

Through laced fingers, Edgar watched as the speaker's telescopic legs moved over him like giant oars. Another ant. Larger than the one he tumbled over, covered in thorns the texture of the rocks that hung overhead.

"You can move now, child," the ant said, pushing the soldier ant to the side with its wedged head.

That must be the Ant King, Edgar thought, standing to face the insects. He stared at his reflection in the large ant's enormous half-domed, obsidian eyes. The soldier ants' heads weren't eyeless—there were two eyes the size of softballs near the center of their heads.

The ants slowly spread open their red-tipped mandibles. Dark vapor burbled from their jaws and as the mist thinned, Edgar knew what he would see next—half a human face. But what he didn't expect were rows upon rows of shark-like teeth.

"Are you the Ant King?" Edgar asked, trying not to stare at their gleaming white teeth.

"I am Lugal, King of Ants. Who are you and why in the worlds would you come down to Kur?"

"My name is Edgar Tooms, sir. Professor Sol Balam sent me. We're in danger. My family's in danger."

"That's unfortunate, but what's that to do with Kur?" the King asked.

"Striders are after us."

"You've seen Striders?"

"Yes, they're after my grandfather. He's a ghost and—"

"A ghost? Gods! You're a Seer!" the Ant King stomped

his feet and broke into laughter. "A Seer's come down to Kur!"

"Yes, Sol said you might be able to help us. We can't fight these things on our own."

"No, I would think not. You're only human and armed with a puny weapon," Lugal snorted.

"Weapon? I don't have a—"

"My antennae smell the Ash of Edom on you, boy," Lugal hissed.

The soldier ant shook its head and snipped at the air with its mandibles. The King fluttered antennae toward his agitated companion. "Now, now, Centurion. This child means us no harm."

"No, of course not. I don't want to hurt you. We just used the Ash to fight off two Striders," Edgar said, raising his enormous palms. They looked like they might float off into the air. "And I was making a paste out of it. There must still be some of it stuck on me."

"You survived a Strider attack? Impressive," Lugal said.

"Just barely. Sol says more are coming. Shadow Striders, I think he called them."

"Then you were right to come here. The Shadow Striders are fanatical butchers with no sense of honor. You'll need soldiers to fight them off. My soldiers."

Edgar hopped up and down. "Yes! That would be amazing. We really need your help."

Lugal snapped his mouthpiece closed and chittered. Moments passed without the ants saying a word. Edgar was confused. Had he said something wrong? Should he have offered to pay the King for his troops. A reward? Show more gratitude?

"Um, sir. Your highness. Will you help us? Do you need anything from me?"

Lugal stomped his feet. The ground rumbled as thousands of craters opened around them. Throbbing explosions erupted on all sides as stalactites came loose from their moorings and crashed to the floor. The jerking motion knocked Edgar to his knees.

"No, there's no need for payment, child. You've already given us a great gift," Lugal shouted over the quake.

"Gift? What gift?" Edgar asked.

Soldier ants crawled out of every crater.

"You tunneled down the Seven Gates to find us. You've made a hole between the worlds that we can climb back from. Don't you see? We're free now."

The trembling faded. Edgar stood and turned in a circle. He was surrounded by thousands, maybe millions of giant ants. They leered at him with their horrible smiles.

Lugal stepped closer to Edgar. "You didn't know this would happen, did you?" He took another step closer. "Tell me again, who was it that sent you?"

"Sol. Professor Sol Balam," Edgar said. "He taught me the chant."

The ant shook its head back and forth in laughter. "The only creature I know who could teach you that song is the traitor, Ugallu."

"Ugallu?" Edgar asked.

"Yes, but that doesn't matter. We're on our way to help you. But be warned, we will snack on any spirit we encounter in your world. So, keep you grandfather close," Lugal said.

"What do I do now?" Edgar asked.

Lugal raised a leg and tapped Edgar's forehead with the tip of his spiny foot, turning the Seer into a cloud of gray mist. A gust of wind swirled Edgar's essence into a funnel and twirled him out of Kur through a hole in the rocky ceiling.

CHAPTER 49
FREE FALLING

Ginnie tumbled through the clouds in a daze. Her outstretched fingers shred the frigid white vapors like a fork through freshly spun cotton candy. Was this a dream? She heard Sol's high-pitched voice in the back of her head, "You've gone ass over tit again, my dear."

She laughed, but the sight of the world rushing up shocked her senses sober. *Definitely not a dream!* The free fall was real, but her mind still didn't understand why it was happening. She was supposed to transport *inside* Edgar's home with Luther and Sharur, not miles above. What went wrong? And what happened to her companions?

All she knew was that if she didn't stop rolling through the sky, she'd throw up. Dying with a vomit-plastered face wasn't an option. Her mind raced as the wind roared in her ears. She'd never parachuted before but had seen videos of grinning idiots who hurled themselves out of perfectly good airplanes and they all looked like they were gliding on their bellies. Maybe that was the thing to do.

She darted her arms and legs out, flattening her body. The cold air pressed against her face and stretched out her red kaftan. The wind thrummed against the fabric like a sail.

"Yes!" Ginnie yelled as her body stabilized. She looked down and smiled. The early evening moon glittered along the Hudson River's choppy surface. Pinpricks of light dotted the shoreline and the patchwork of dull green and brown below.

Faint honks turned to shrieks as she dropped through a formation of geese. Passing safely, she focused on the ground again. Her heart drummed against her chest as the sounds of traffic grew louder.

"Ginevra! Help me!" a voice shouted.

To her right, Luther tumbled through the sky. *Had he been there the entire time?* The scorpion clawed at the air, desperate to find something to latch onto. He looked terrified.

"I'm so sorry!" she yelled. Tears, like shimmering beads of mercury, raced into the corners of her wind-beaten eyes.

A dark, slender shape sped across her vision. Twak!

What felt like a plank of wood struck her across the stomach, knocking the wind out of her. *Sharur!*

"I've got you!" the staff grunted, slowing Ginnie's descent. "Swing your legs over and straddle on."

Ginnie flew through the air like a witch, clutching Sharur so hard that her hands turned white.

"We need to save Luther," Sharur said, arching toward the scorpion. She nodded, unable to speak, barely able to breathe.

Luckily, Ginnie only had to hold on as they sped

toward Luther. The scorpion had splayed his body out and curled in its stinger to let Sharur and Ginnie safely approach.

"Clasp onto my pommel!" Sharur shouted, keeping level with Luther's descent. The scorpion reached out and snapped his claw around Sharur's pommel, grasping only air.

"Try again! We don't have much time!"

Sharur was right. The town grew larger with every passing moment. Luther's claws glided off the smooth metal again. Ginnie craned her neck back for a better look, but Luther had sunk below her line of sight. She heard a sharp clank as an enormous weight pulled Sharur vertical. She hugged the staff with all her strength to keep from slipping as they slowed to a stop.

She opened her eyes. They were floating above the church now. She glanced down and shuddered as she considered how close she was to being impaled on the church spire's copper crucifix. Luther's human mouth, three times the size of hers, smiled as it held onto Sharur with one claw.

"Ha! We did it!" Luther shouted. "Any chance we could get back down to solid ground now?"

Sharur slowly descended, hovering in front of the church's wooden double doors. Luther let go and landed on the stone path. He raised his claws and Ginnie stepped down, placing a foot on each pincer. She wobbled on his slick shell and hopped off, landing in a squatted position. Ginnie stood and stretched, happy to be on solid ground.

"Why isn't anyone looking at us?" she asked, staring at the handful of late-night commuters marching home from the train station by the river. They walked past in a post-work haze, many of their eyes glued to the small glowing phones in their hands. But someone should have seen their fall or noticed the blue scorpion the size of a Ford Fiesta by Ginnie's side.

"We're still cloaked by the travel tablet. It's how Striders are able to move around the worlds without being seen," Sharur said, floating next to Ginnie. "The illusion won't last long for us though—we can't control it like they can."

"Why didn't we appear inside Edgar's house?" Luther asked.

"I don't know. Maybe the operator made a mistake. She did seem nervous," Sharur said.

Luther snapped at the staff with his claw. "Maybe you shouldn't have threatened to gut her family."

Sharur rolled his eyes. "We can still get to the boy's home from here, can't we?"

"Yeah, it's about a ten-minute walk." She pointed up the street. "We go straight up, pass the grocery store, and take a left on Warburton."

"Good. Let's get marching! I don't want to be out in the open when our invisibility runs out," Luther said.

Ginnie groaned.

"What's wrong?" Luther asked.

"Mind if I ride on one of you guys? That was one hell of a trip, and I'm so damn tired."

Sharur laughed and angled lower. "Sure, hop on."

CHAPTER 50
EVENING STROLL

Ginnie's eyes burned with exhaustion. Her grip on the staff slackened, and she almost fell off as Sharur sped silently through town. She squeezed her thighs tighter around Sharur and straightened her back.

Luther scurried a few feet below on her right. His thin, nimble legs scuttled over concrete and asphalt. Occasionally, he'd veer off and lunge for a pigeon only to rejoin their procession empty-clawed and annoyed.

Aunt Ginnie smiled and tilted her head back. The night air ran its cool fingers through her long hair. As they crossed Cedar Street, the sounds of village nightlife washed over her—music, utensils clattering on ceramic dishes, diners laughing, children crying, the sound of traffic whooshing over pavement.

They left the sound of the town center behind for cicadas chittering, dogs barking, and, in the distance, a ship's foghorn echoing across the Hudson River.

Her chin drooped and the streetlights blurred into a whirl of light. *I'll just take a little power nap,* she thought.

Sharur knew what street to turn on, the house number, and—thump!

Ginnie landed in the grass.

Sharur turned himself upright and laughed. "You fell asleep."

Ginnie smiled and tried standing up. Her head felt heavy and she panicked. *Am I still a deformed mess?* She looked down at her hands and exhaled in relief. *Normal!* She patted her body and exhaled.

Sharur grunted, steam billowed from his nostrils. "Are you ok? Did you hit your head?"

"No, no. I'm just thrilled that I still look human." She stood up and faced Sharur. She was surprised to meet his gaze straight on.

"Did you shrink? You're shorter now," she said, standing with her back to the staff. She waved a hand above her head and felt the top edge of Sharur's horns. "You're the same height as me now."

"As I said, most things have to change between the worlds, and I am not immune to these phenomena."

Ginnie turned around. "Hey, where'd Luther go?"

A clump of towering forsythia bushes rustled. Without thinking, Ginnie grabbed Sharur and pointed the ox head toward the fluttering leaves as two enormous claws parted the greenery like curtains.

"Luther! You scared the hell out of us!" Ginnie shouted. She stumbled backward as the scorpion made his way out.

Unlike the staff, Luther didn't shrink. He remained the size of a small car. His blue shell shimmered in the moonlight and the mesmerizing stinger bobbed high in the air.

"Luther, did you hear me?" Ginnie asked, slowly lowering her gaze. The scorpion had something in its mouth. She focused her eyes and immediately regretted being so curious.

Luther's mandibles were stuffed with fur as they pinched and cut into a striped gray mass. Blood oozed from the lacerations and dripped on the grass. A small leather collar slipped out and flapped in the air.

"What?" Luther slurped in the pink leather. Twang! Out popped a wad of metal that landed by Ginnie's feet. She picked up the heart-shaped medallion and gasped. The inscription read, Cardi.

"Jesus! Luther, did you just eat a cat?"

The scorpion raised his claws, blocking Ginnie's view of his mouth pieces. Something crunched and squelched behind the scorpion's pincers.

"What's a cat?" Luther slurred.

"Give him a minute," Sharur said, slipping out of Ginnie's grip. "He's digesting the creature in his mouth."

"Christ, we don't have time for this," Ginnie said, waving her hands trying to clear the image of the half-masticated cat from her vision like a bad odor.

"So sorry about that," Luther said, finishing his meal. He turned toward the house, coughed, and pointed a claw at the front door. "Is this the Seer's home?"

"Yeah, this is Edgar's house. At least, I hope it is. I've only been inside once," she said.

"This is the address you gave me," Sharur said.

"Well, is anyone home?" Luther asked.

"Let's find out." Ginnie walked up the porch steps and knocked on the door. She heard movement and voices, but no one answered. She stepped over and peered into one of the front windows. Luther clambered behind her and looked through the other window.

"Do you two see anything?" Sharur asked.

Ginnie was about to answer, but a low growl turned her attention. Across the street, a snow-white terrier sat on its haunches snarling at the trio. Its corded leash was held by a young woman in neon jogging clothes. The woman raised a hand as if to wave hello and paused.

Sharur did say their invisibility wouldn't last much longer. Ginnie waited for a B-horror movie scream to fill the air, but it never came. Instead, the woman rubbed her eyes with the back of her hand and shook her head. Even the dog lost interest and licked its privates before it was tugged away into the night.

"That was close," Ginnie said. She turned the door-knob. Locked. "We need to get inside before someone does spot us."

"Why don't we go around to the backyard? Maybe a back door is open," Ginnie said.

"Sounds like a good idea," Luther said, scuttling forward.

CHAPTER 51

VOYEURS

Ginnie pressed her forehead against the living room window. She didn't understand why her niece, Sol, Margaret, and Charles's floating head were all standing around in a semicircle gazing at the carpet.

"God, that's weird," Ginnie said.

"What? You mean the ghost?" Sharur asked, nodding at Charles. "They usually emanate their entire body, not just a head. That only happens when there's been an—"

Ginnie waved her hand. "No, no. I've met Charles. I just don't understand why they're all just . . . waiting."

Ginnie banged on the window and shouted. No one turned.

"Let's try that back door," Sharur suggested.

"No, look!" Ginnie whispered, as black flecks swirled and formed into a boy's shape on the living room floor. The motes flashed brightly and Edgar Tooms reappeared.

Luther hissed.

Ginnie slowly turned around. The scorpion's body trembled. A drop of clear fluid splashed onto his hard back. Ginnie looked up and saw Luther's quivering stinger. The black-tipped talon glistened with viscous venom.

"Luther, what's wrong? Why are you so . . . angry?"

"The boy!" Luther snarled. "The boy's used the last travel tablet!"

"What are you talking about?" Sharur asked.

"Look at the boy's hands!"

Ginnie and Sharur turned their attention back to the scene. It took a moment for everyone surrounding Edgar to move away, but then they saw his mud-covered hands.

"Oh, my Lords," Sharur said.

Ginnie shook her head. "I don't understand. What's wrong?"

"Sol must have given Edgar the last travel tablet!" Luther rubbed his claws together so hard sparks ignited. "Don't you see? The clay's melted!"

"Ok, sure. But what's all that mean?" Ginnie asked.

"It means we're trapped here, in the land of the living!" Luther said.

A commotion inside the room stole Ginnie's attention. Edgar shoved Sol. *What in the world was happening?*

"We have to get in there," Ginnie said.

"Damn right, we have to—"

"No, Luther. I need you to stay out here. I don't think anyone in that house is prepared to see a giant pissed off scorpion stomp into the living room."

"Fine, but I want answers," Luther snarled.

Ginnie nodded, grabbed Sharur, and rushed to the back door, hoping for a happy reunion.

CHAPTER 52
BACK HOME

From the darkness, someone screamed. Edgar didn't actually hear the shouts—he had no ears—he was still a formless being, stuck between Kur and his world, the land of the living.

The yelling continued, agitating the billions of tiny dust motes that now made up his essence, drawing them closer and closer until a faint outline of his body appeared in the living room. The outline darkened, stiffened, and Edgar materialized as if turned on like a light switch.

Edgar stared at his goo-covered hands.

A thick brown batter oozed down his wrists and plopped onto the carpet. What was he holding that could have melted like this? A giant chocolate bar? He hated milk chocolate.

Images of cuneiform flashed across his mind. He blinked hard. No, it wasn't a chocolate bar, but it was something square, like . . . a tablet! Yes! Edgar remembered holding the travel tablet Sol had given him. *Where was the professor?* He had to tell them about the ants. There were so many of them. Had he dreamed it? His bones ached and there was so much he couldn't remember.

Edgar looked up. He was surrounded by his mother, Clara, Sol, and Opa Chuck. Their mouths moved, but he couldn't hear a word over the sound of screaming. His vision blurred as Margaret shook him by his shoulders. He tried reading her lips, but they moved so slowly. Then Edgar recognized the hysterical voice—it was his own.

"Snap out of it, Edgar! You're back. You're back home," Margaret said. She gripped his shoulders even harder.

Edgar winced and met her gaze. His scream trailed off from his O-shaped mouth.

"Mom?" he croaked.

"Yes, honey. It's me. You're ok . . . you're ok," she said, hugging Edgar.

Edgar had never been happier to see his mother. He wrapped his arms around her and squeezed. *Thank God*, he thought. A sense of relief washed over him as the smell of coffee and stale cigars wafted between him and his mother.

Sol squatted close by and smiled. "Well, what did the Ant King say?"

Edgar broke away from his mother and drove his palms into Sol's chest. The old man toppled on his back.

"What in the world? Why did you do that?" Opa Chuck asked, fluttering over to Sol.

The professor stood and waved Charles away. "It's ok. The boy has every reason to be upset." Sol picked at the wet clay prints Edgar's hands left behind on his suit and flicked a glob at Edgar. "That shove, however, was unnecessary and childish."

"Why didn't you tell me what was going to happen to me?" Edgar asked, wiping the mud off his cheek.

"I did. More or less. I told you it wasn't going to be easy or comfortable."

"But you didn't say anything about how I would change. How I'd transform or what I'd do just by going down there," Edgar shot back.

"Well, for one, you might not have gone. And there was no way to know with certainty that your traveling down to Kur would actually free the Myrmidon. It was a possibility. Really, a long shot, but—"

Edgar's mother stepped between the two. She faced Edgar and stroked his face. "Honey, what happened?"

"My body changed. I changed. It was horrible," Edgar said. "And there were these ants, Mom. Giant ants the size of pickup trucks, and their mouths, the ones inside their mouths, had shark teeth!"

"That sounds awful—"

"What did the Ant King say?" Sol asked.

"Christ! Why can't you just give him a minute? The poor boy's obviously been through—" Charles started to say, but Edgar stomped forward.

"The Ant King says they're on their way up, Ugallu."

Sol raised an eyebrow.

"What? Does that name sound familiar, professor?" Sol's title hissed out from between Edgar's clenched teeth.

The back door opened with a click. Edgar turned.

Footsteps and thudding followed. It sounded as though someone was driving a pole into the ground with every other step. A cold knot bloomed in Edgar's stomach. They had dropped their guard, and the creatures picked this moment to attack.

This was my fault, he thought.

He glanced at Clara and wondered why she was smiling.

CHAPTER 53
STRANGE REUNION

Edgar rubbed his eyes. Aunt Ginnie was back! Her hair radiated out in every direction as if someone had rubbed a balloon around her head. She held a strange metal staff— the top part looked like a cow's head or some kind of bull. For a moment, Edgar thought it blinked, but then Clara rushed past.

"Tía! You're back!" she shouted, jumping into Aunt Ginnie's arms.

Aunt Ginnie squeezed and planted a barrage of kisses on her niece's face. Clara laughed and wrapped her arms around her aunt's neck. They rocked back and forth as tears streamed down both their faces.

Clara sniffled. "I thought I lost you. I saw you disappear."

"I know, honey. I know." Aunt Ginnie wiped her own tears away with the back of her hand. "But I made it back from that awful place."

"Ginevra? Is that you?" Sol asked. He took off his sunglasses and smiled.

"In the flesh, Sol," Ginnie said. She let go of her niece and glared at the professor. "Now, Sol, you have some explaining to do. Why don't we start with why you've made Edgar here so angry?"

"Well, we just had a little disagreement—"

Edgar's anger flared again. "A little disagreement? A little disagreement! I almost died in Kur!"

"So that's what happened to the travel tablet. You sent the boy to see the Myrmidon!" Sharur said.

Edgar's jaw dropped. He turned and glanced at everyone's faces. They all had the same shocked expression.

"Did your walking stick just talk?" Charles asked.

Sharur levitated and floated into the center of the room.

"I am no walking stick, sir. My name is—"

"Sharur! You must be Sharur!" Clara said.

"They do know of me in this world!" Sharur said, spinning around to face Clara.

Sol laughed. "No, my friend. I've told them a little bit about you."

The professor turned his gaze back to Aunt Ginnie. "Ginevra, it's so good to see you. Luther said he was making his way back with you."

Aunt Ginnie wrapped her arms around Sol. The old man almost disappeared in the bear hug. She held his face between her palms and they kissed. "You crazy old bastard."

"Ahem," Charles grunted.

"Sorry about that. I just never thought I'd make it back home," Aunt Ginnie said. "And it's so good to see my Sol again. We used to date."

Edgar huffed. He didn't appreciate how everyone's

attention had drifted away from what just happened to him—from what Sol did to him.

Edgar caught a glimpse of something moving behind Aunt Ginnie. He was about to shout a warning when his mother screamed as an enormous claw pushed Aunt Ginnie to the side. A blur of legs and pincers scrambled into the room. A huge tail swung in an arc, knocking everyone down.

Edgar held his stomach and struggled to breathe. A scorpion. A giant blue scorpion, who pinned Sol's neck to the wall in the crook of its enormous, hairy claw.

"Hello, Luther," Sol gurgled. He hammered at the scorpion's claw with his fists. "It's nice to see you again, my friend."

"You lied! You said you'd give me your last travel tablet," Luther snarled.

"I know. I'm so sorry, but we didn't have a choice. There was no way to know if you were actually going to make it before Cressida and her Shadow Striders arrived," Sol said.

Luther drove the points of his pincers deeper into the wall. Sol struggled to breathe as his legs jerked in the air. Edgar relished Sol's pain, but anxiety crawled up his spine. What would they do without Sol when the Striders came back? Something cracked and Edgar's attention snapped back to the fight in front of him.

"But why let the boy use it?" Luther asked.

"I sent him to Kur," Sol said.

"Are you insane? You sent Edgar—a Seer—down to Kur?" Luther pulled his claw out of the wall and Sol fell to the floor. "You've let loose an army of psychopaths. They'll flood our world and force every six-legged Phantid to their side. It'll be a civil war."

Sol massaged his neck. "Yes, but Lugal's agreed to help us here. We can survive with his soldier ants on our side."

"Really? There's a good chance that the Myrmidon will turn on all of us after they kill the Shadow Striders. You have a plan for that?"

Sol rubbed his neck. "What choice did I have?"

"Why are we all arguing?" Sharur boomed. "There's probably a Strider scout already here, watching us, and reporting back to General Cressida."

"Sharur's right," Sol said. "We need to finish our preparations for the invasion. And with our friends here, we have a fighting chance." Sol glared at Luther. "We have friends here, don't we?"

Luther raised his claw. "Yes, of course you do. What choice do any of us have now, eh?"

"So, what do we do?" Clara asked.

"Yeah, what's the plan?" Edgar said.

Everyone turned to face Sol. The professor coughed again and smoothed out his suit. "The first thing we do is to start spreading all that flour Margaret collected into Zisurrûs. That's the easy part."

"What's the hard part?"

"Making a diorama."

CHAPTER 54
THE MZ

Malva rumbled through the Rookery's corridors raging at the Marquis. Her thin, bowed legs pumped like train pistons. Clods of packed earth erupted as her four spiked feet speared the ground, leaving a path of three-toed craters in their wake.

Striders traveling in both directions flattened themselves along the tunnel's curved sides as Malva thundered by.

"It's not fair! It's not fair!" she hissed. Bursts of dark pneuma jetted through her mouths and trailed like squid ink.

An image of Clara's angry face flashed in Malva's mind. She raised her claws as the memory of burning Ash flooded her vision. Malva tripped and crashed against the wall. The breathing pores lining her long abdomen opened and closed rapidly like hairy barnacles.

"Are you ok?" Andrés asked, skulking closer. He stretched out his hooked claws.

She'd forgotten he was crawling behind her. This was

the second time in as many days that she'd appeared weak in front of the smaller hunter.

"I'm fine!" Malva swatted Andrés's claws away, lumbering back to a standing position. "Come on. General Cressida's waiting for us."

Gods, the humiliation! she thought. She'd never been placed under anyone's command. Never! She ran a claw against the wall, etching a jagged groove into the glazed tile work. The lights flickered as she sliced through a group of fireflies clamped on stone near the top edge of the tunnel.

"Could you stop doing that? The screeching is unbearable," Andrés said.

"It's not fair, Andrés! It's not my fault those little mites had the Ash of Edom. There was no way for us to know," Malva said. "And now we have to report to General Cressida?"

Malva flicked the lightning bug's luminous white blood from her claw and faced Andrés. "I'm the Ghost Scythe! Do you know how many of my uncle's enemies I've assassinated? I don't take orders like a common grunt!"

"Well, the Marquis said we had to—"

"I know what Uncle said!"

Andrés looked away and rubbed his claws together.

Malva marched forward, taking a steep path toward the Rookery's famed MZ—the Military Zone. The corridor widened and the elaborate tessellated tile work gave way to thick stucco where carved images of Striders in battle jutted out from the wall. Glowing mushrooms lined the floor, casting a dull blue light against the life-size sculptures.

"I don't see what's so special about this place," Malva said. She stopped to stare at a wall full of roaring Strider soldiers. Their feet clasped down on severed beetle heads. "They seem quite full of themselves."

Andrés shrugged. "I don't know. It'd be nice if there were at least a few mosaics celebrating us hunters. We're the ones powering and feeding the Rookery, you know?"

He wasn't wrong, Malva thought. Hunters were treated like disposable workers in Irkalla. She didn't envy Andrés's social position. *Would he survive this mission? Would Uncle even let him live?* A small part of her hoped so. She watched him lower his head to examine a clay tablet embedded on the wall.

"This is old. Very old," he said. "The inscription is in a Phantid Akkadian hybrid."

"What's it say?"

"Sho Shum Saragon." Andrés cocked his head to the side. "At least that's what I think it says. What's that supposed to mean?"

Malva laughed. "It literally means, give your claw to the Marquis."

Andrés's pupils narrowed. "Give your claw?"

"Place your trust in the Marquis is what we would say nowadays. Our ancestors were a bit more dramatic with language." A steady drumming in the distance drew her attention. She turned her back on Andrés and scuttled toward where the tunnel flared open.

Malva looked down the slanted drop at the huge circular field below. The flat ground was covered in glossy bitumen. Enormous cuneiform symbols were painted white along the surface—they reminded Malva of airport runways in the human world.

"This place is huge. It's at least the same width as the Rookery's base—miles and miles across." Andrés pointed a claw at the Strider troops massed along the outer edge. "That looks like fun."

Malva grinned. Hundreds of Strider troops, arranged in wedge formations, marched in the distance. She counted a dozen formations with at least seventy-five soldiers to a single wedge just within her line of sight.

The troops looped clockwise around the periphery of the field's edge, circling hundreds of mud bunkers that looked like dung heaps. At the very center of the circular arena sat a massive purple glass dome. Thick stone struts formed the hexagonal lattices that lined its curved surface. The structure looked like a colossal insect eye.

Andrés stared at the same spot.

Malva pointed a claw toward the structure. "That's General Cressida's headquarters."

"That's where we're going, isn't it?"

Malva nodded and started down the steep descent. She heard Andrés grunt and the sound of his feet pattering closely behind. The Strider soldiers marching by didn't give them a second glance as they moved toward the center of the field.

"Gods, this place is depressing . . . and cold," Malva said as white vapor bloomed from her breath. She followed the tendrils upward and marveled at the chamber's cooling gills—rows of sheets made from hardened mud spiraled around the high ceiling in tightening concentric rows.

Stubby, mutated glowworms crawled along the flat surfaces, casting a dull red glow from cancerous growths along their bodies. Their tiny feet scraped at layers of gritty frost that floated to the ground like snowflakes.

Malva shivered and pushed forward. She could see the dome's entrance, an enormous stone slab just a few yards away, when two Shadow Strider guards stepped in front of her path. Had they always been standing there? They seemed to have sprouted from the building's shadow.

Malva's bulbous eyes strained to focus on their shapes. Their slick, sinuous exoskeletons were the color of crude oil and perfectly smooth. Gods, so smooth! Malva couldn't see a single segment on their sleek husks.

Patches of brown fur flared from their backs and ran like flames along their thin arms. Their blood-red mandibles spread open, startling Malva with their small human mouths—children!

"You're the Marquis's niece? The Ghost Scythe?" they asked with high-pitched, lilting voices.

Malva's single antenna twitched. Their menacing appearance and gentle tones unnerved her more than anything she'd recently encountered in the worlds.

"We're here to see General Cressida," Malva said. She glanced back at Andrés who had tightened his body as small as possible. He looked like a quivering bamboo pole.

The back casings of the guards spread open, flaring out their translucent wings. The stone door behind them slid inward. The Shadow Striders bowed and stepped to the side, giving Malva and Andrés a path to enter.

Andrés walked closely along her side as she stepped forward. As uncomfortable as she felt, she knew this was a thousand times worse for the hunter. Every warrior in the MZ was female, at least twice the size of Andrés. And they were all kept on strict rations—even the Shadow Striders.

If Andrés wandered into the zone on his own, he would be devoured. Malva laughed as the two guards licked their lips.

She wrapped a claw around her partner and pushed him forward. "Come on, let's get on with it."

CHAPTER 55

GENERAL CRESSIDA

Malva stepped into the ill-lit dome. Hardly any light from the worms or luminescent mushrooms outside penetrated the purple glass. Tiny feet scuttled and scraped on the smooth stone nearby. She felt surrounded. A quick glance left and right confirmed they weren't alone. Barely visible Shadow Striders lined the walls of General Cressida's inner sanctum like solemn statues.

The air crackled with electricity as two enormous fireflies ignited. Malva and Andrés shielded their eyes with the wide, flat edges of their curved claws. As the flash faded, Malva caught a glimpse of the general at the far end of the circular room—tall, spindly, and the color of freshly tilled earth. Her exoskeleton was covered in bumpy nodes, like armored gooseflesh.

When the fireflies' abdomens flared again, she was gone. The luminous beasts had turned lengthwise with their heads facing opposite directions. Streams of light crackled and arched between their rumps. The veins of light thickened and stretched into a taut membrane of energy.

"Oh, it's time for a picture show," Malva grumbled. She hoped that one day their world would adopt human technology like film projectors. Seeing images displayed using Crawlers like this seemed inefficient.

A flickering image of Edgar Tooms's home appeared on the phosphorescent screen stretched between the two bugs. The house turned on an invisible carousel, giving Malva and Andrés a 360-degree view. A tiny, human-shaped shadow appeared in the attic window with a small glob hovering over its shoulder.

"That's the Seer and the ghost!" Andrés said. "Is this happening now?"

Static fizzled over the image and then disappeared as General Cressida's legs stepped through the screen. Malva and Andrés looked up.

"She's a colossus," Malva whispered. If this was the human world, she'd compare Cressida to a telephone pole. Maybe her conical head wouldn't reach the very top, but it'd be close.

"No, that was recorded by a Strider Scout not long after your first failure, Andrés." Cressida lowered her head and wrapped her thick segmented antennae around the hunter's neck. The antennae uncoiled with a snap as the general turned her attention to Malva.

"You! I know who your uncle is," Cressida snarled. "And I don't care. The Marquis placed you under my command, and you'll do as I say."

Malva hissed and raised her claws. The Shadow Striders lining the walls marched forward, encircling Malva and Andrés.

"My partner here means no disrespect." Andrés bowed and tapped Malva's side. "She's just unaccustomed to the . . . chain of command, General."

The bastard wants me to bow? Malva could barely contain her anger.

Please, Andrés mouthed.

He looked pitiful in this demeaned state. But the little hunter's instincts were well-founded. They were in a precarious situation—thirty of the Rookery's most elite warriors and the general giantess were more than Malva could handle. She'd meet Andrés and Cressida halfway. Malva's thin legs bent slightly as she curtsied.

"Good. Now that we understand each other, we can move forward. You'll be part of my thirty-strong strike team," General Cressida said.

"That's it? Thirty Shadow Striders? We're dealing with a Seer here—"

"A boy. We're dealing with a human child that happens to be a Seer, an inexperienced one at that. He has no support, besides the female child, and no weapons of note."

"They have the Ash of Edom," Malva said, "who knows what else—"

"We're going in with the thirty Shadow Striders you see around you. We'll overwhelm the children with a simultaneous strike in every room of the house. From the basement to the attic, they'll have nowhere to hide. We have superior numbers and the element of surprise."

"B-but, General the boy's a Seer. He hurt me." Andrés raised the claw Edgar had clasped onto. He turned it so General Cressida could see the barely healed, hand-shaped crater.

Cressida laughed. "Andrés, you're just a hunter. No offense to you or your profession, but all you've had to deal with over the centuries are skittish ghosts that can't fight back. My Shadow Striders are trained soldiers. I can see how a human child could land a lucky strike on a hunter. What I don't understand is how the famed Ghost Scythe was taken by surprise by the young female."

Malva growled. "I was in the middle of transformation—"

"An unnecessary spectacle that almost cost you your life!" Cressida interrupted. "As I said, my soldiers are professionals. They don't toy with their victims. This will be a surgical strike. We'll be in and out before the humans realize what happened."

General Cressida twitched her antennae. "I'm sending you our battle plans now."

A mental image of Edgar's home slammed into Malva's thoughts followed by a dream sequence of how the general imagined the strike would unfold. She was right. It was a good plan.

"Do either of you have any questions?"

"No, ma'am," they said.

"Good, then you two are dismissed. Meet me in the teleportation chambers in fifteen. There'll be a battle hymn ceremony before we go."

Andrés grunted.

"It's tradition," General Cressida said. "Besides, the Marquis insists."

CHAPTER 56
ALTERNATE PLANS

Andrés couldn't shake the feeling that something was terribly wrong with General Cressida's plan. The thought rattled in his brain as he followed Malva out of the MZ.

The fact that the children had the Ash of Edom meant they had access to skills long forgotten in the human realm. They'd either come across it by chance, as the Marquis suggested, or they had help—expert help.

He scurried closer to Malva. She seemed lost in her own thoughts. "I think we're walking into a trap," he said.

The Ghost Scythe stopped.

"It's the Ash," he said. "There's something else at play here."

"I've been thinking the same thing, Andrés."

"What should we do? I don't think the general's going to—"

"If something were to happen to General Cressida when we land . . ." Malva paused and twirled her claw in the air. ". . . would you nominate me to take command?"

Andrés considered the question. If General Cressida

fell, the next highest-ranking Shadow Strider would, under normal circumstances, take over, but Malva was royalty. Her status would only supersede the chain of command temporarily.

"It could work, but those troops are loyal to their own. You'd have to take care of any dissenters."

"You let me worry about that." Malva turned. "But you'd support my nomination?"

Andrés nodded.

Suddenly, Malva's head was just below his. The tips of her mandibles gently clamped onto his neck stalk. He raised his claws, but she pressed them down with her larger forelimbs.

A slow hiss slithered out of her two mouths. The smell of overripe mangos filled the air. When he first met Malva, he would have given his right claw to be this close to her, but now all he wanted was another world—or two—between him and the Ghost Scythe.

"Good. Don't you dare disappoint me when the time comes," Malva growled.

"I-I won't."

She responded by pinching tighter. *This is it,* Andrés thought. *This is how I'm going to die.* It's how most males of his species met their end, so it shouldn't have surprised him. Andrés turned his head up and focused on the ceiling.

The cold grasp of Malva's mandibles vanished. Andrés's antennae stiffened. They caught another scent in the air—pheromones. *Gods this is confusing,* he thought, but dared not look down. He didn't peek until Malva's rump slid under his legs.

"Quickly," she said. "We only have a few minutes."

CHAPTER 57
BATTLE PREPARATIONS

Edgar's eyeball slowly eclipsed the attic window like a green alien moon. He imagined his miniature self gazing in horror at an enormous black pupil. He laughed and stepped back to admire the model home Sol and Clara had crafted from little more than shoeboxes, glue, fabric scraps, and plastic bricks. His mom, Opa, Aunt Ginnie, and their new allies, Luther and Sharur, stood around the coffee table in the living room, gazing at the whimsical diorama set on a field of green construction paper.

"This is amazing, you guys!" Edgar squatted and peered into another window. "You even made furniture from leftover cardboard!"

"That's not the best part," Sol said. He turned to face his art collaborator. "Clara, why don't you show everyone what you did?"

She grasped the edges and spread the model open on a center hinge. A round of oohs and aahs spread from everyone as the interior of the home flared out.

"I think it's some of my best work." Clara smiled and

flicked off imaginary dust from her shoulders. "It's an accurate 1:18 scale model of Casa Tooms. Sol wanted to go 1:12, but I thought that was overkill. Besides, we didn't even have time to paint this one."

"It's beautiful, Clara, but I still don't understand how this is going to help us," Margaret said.

"That's for me to explain," Sol said, stepping forward, cradling a shoebox. A small, muscular green limb poked out from a hole in the side. The professor dropped the box on the table; the contents rattled and rolled about inside.

As Sol lifted the cover, Edgar smiled at the sight of some of his old toys—ninja turtles, an old rat in a karate outfit, a Ken doll head, a windup ladybug, and a Mickey Mouse figurine, all laying on a bed of black beans.

"Each one of these toys represents one of us," Sol said. He pointed to the turtles. "Margaret, Ginnie, and Clara are these green mutant creatures. The severed head is obviously Charles. I'm the wise old rat, and this well-dressed fellow with the big ears is—"

"Mickey Mouse. I'm Mickey. I get the joke, professor." Edgar shivered, remembering his recent transformation as a necronaut. "You're a real jerk, you know?"

Luther grunted in agreement as Sol grinned.

"Ah! Almost forgot!" Clara whipped out a black Sharpie marker from her cargo pant pocket and leaned it against the house. "That's supposed to be Sharur."

"Good, now we can begin." Sol placed the figures throughout the miniature house with the care and determination of a chess grandmaster. Once finished, he closed the two halves of the home and turned it so the back of the house faced the group.

The professor uncapped the marker and drew a series

of nested curves around the front yard and backyard. Edgar recognized the lines as the magic flour circles they had poured earlier. Since they were working in teams, he hadn't realized how much of the outside they covered with the stuff. Sol's dark squiggles looked like a force field.

Sol reached back into the empty box and scooped out a handful of beans.

"These little bastards are the Shadow Striders." Sol let the beans fall onto the paper. As they spun on their hard shells, Edgar's heart sank. The black beans looked like an unstoppable army compared to the seven action figures huddled in the diorama.

"All the Zisurrûs we've cast inside and around the house using the flour will block Striders from teleporting in and force them to appear at the far end of the back-yard." The professor pushed the black mass into a pile with his palms. He pinched one bean between his thumb and forefinger and flicked it at the house. "Obviously, a few will try to fly through the windows, but they'll bounce off. And Gods, will they be confused!"

A dagger-thin smile crept across Sol's wrinkled face. He stabbed the green paper with the Sharpie so it looked like a mad connect-the-dots puzzle.

"I'll need everyone to fill up the balloons with Ash and stake them in the yard. Once the Striders get their bear-ings, they'll try rushing the house. The balloons are going to act like landmines and force them onto the only safe path that leads into the house."

"Why? Why give them a way inside?" Charles asked.

"So we can force them into a tight corridor—this killing zone." Sol ran a finger from the pile of beans toward the back door. He tapped the model home's second-floor bedroom window. "Margaret, I'm placing you up there with the nail gun. You had the best aim during our impromptu target practice earlier. The moment you see the Striders march into the zone, I want you to open fire. You'll have no trouble hitting your targets."

"Do you think we'll be able to kill all of them?" Edgar asked.

"No, but we'll thin out their numbers. More than a few are going to make it into the house, and we'll have to fight them in here." Sol opened the diorama. "We'll set up a few more traps for them at the back door."

"Wait! What do I do when I'm out of nails?" Margaret asked.

"Head back to your bedroom with me, Clara, Ginnie, and Edgar. We'll be armed with Ash-coated spears." He pointed to the ninja turtles holding their plastic weapons —Clara had coated the tips of the bō staff, twin katana, and twin sais with dollops of white paint.

"What's to stop them from coming into the bedroom?"

"Luther," Sol said, matter-of-factly. He picked up a ladybug toy from the box and turned its winding key. The plastic insect rattled back and forth along the model home's second-floor landing. "Luther's our second line of defense. He'll stop any Striders coming up the stairs."

"For how long?" Luther asked.

"For as long as you can, my friend. We don't know when the Myrmidon are coming so we'll need to slow down our enemies for as long as possible."

"What if something happens to Luther?" Aunt Ginnie asked.

"Then we'll all rush up to the attic and link up with Charles and Sharur. We'll make our stand there," Sol said.

"Wait, why in the world am I up in the attic with Sharur?" Charles asked.

"Unfortunately, there's nothing you can do to defend yourself, Mr. Tooms. Sharur is the strongest among us, and he'll be able to protect you from any threat," Sol said.

"If Sharur's so powerful, why can't we just have him, you know, kill everyone?" Clara asked.

"I'm strong, but not invincible," Sharur said. "Besides, I see what Sol's doing. If everything goes according to plan, there'll be little of the Striders left for me to deal with. This might work."

"I have to agree. It's doubtful that General Cressida's planned for any kind of resistance," Luther added. "You have to remember, there hasn't been a Seer in thousands of years. These Striders are used to having their way and they'll be underestimating all of us."

Edgar hoped Luther was right.

CHAPTER 58
INTO THE BREACH

"Is this your first time?" Malva asked.

Andrés was speechless. He never expected to survive a coupling or step inside the Royal Teleportation Terminal. The day was full of surprises.

His bulbous eyes tracked the hundreds of Striders crawling in and out of the teleportation chambers. They seemed so carefree in their travels. It wasn't fair. Day in and day out, hunters like him had to march through Irkalla's deserts to move between the worlds. It was exhausting.

Malva turned her head. "Well?"

"Yeah. First time here," he finally answered. "We're not allowed to use the Royal Teleportation Terminal."

"I've never understood that rule," Malva said, staring at the fireflies skittering across the vaulted ceiling.

"It's tradition." Andrés sighed. "Something about keeping the purity of the hunt intact. A load of beetle dung if you ask me. These fine royals just don't want us working rabble around. Honestly, we'd be able to bring back our orbs faster if we could just step through one of those arches."

"Well, if this all works out, I'll make sure Uncle gives you a pass or some kind of promotion, Andrés," Malva said.

"That would be nice. I appreciate the—"

Something bumped into Andrés's rear right foot. Then the left. Andrés's pupils widened into disks at the sight of a massive red centipede weaving under his four bowed legs. Its rippling body was as thick as a birch tree and it carried a wooden lute strapped to its back.

Malva hissed as another centipede, just as large, wriggled past her. It joined its undulating twin farther ahead, speeding toward the traffic controller's hut. Just beyond the brass booth, Andrés caught a glimpse of General Cressida towering in the distance.

"The far end of the terminal is reserved for military use," Malva said. She scuttled ahead, knocking a few Striders to the side as she sped forward. Andrés followed in her wake.

As they approached the military transport chambers, Andrés noticed a black cloud hovering in front of a long mud-brick stage. Within a few steps, however, he realized that the darkness was really a line of Shadow Striders standing at attention with their serrated forelimbs and legs tucked tightly against their bodies. They swayed side to side like black wheat stalks.

"You made it just in time, Andrés," General Cressida said, pointing at the stage.

Andrés stared at the two elephant-sized Atlas beetles just a few feet away. The dumb beasts were on their backs. Their thin legs wiggled in the air. Why in the worlds would they position themselves that way? A moment later, Andrés had his answer.

A thin, elderly mantis emerged from behind a red velvet curtain. Its ashen exoskeleton seemed impossibly soft, as if it was made from leather instead of hard chitin. Long, brown antennae drooped from the tip of his cylinder-shaped head and trailed behind gangly legs.

"It's a Gray Claw," Andrés whispered. He'd never seen one before. He'd heard stories, of course, about these millennia-old Striders who had fought with Isimud. The chances of seeing one now were astronomical.

Andrés sucked in a breath of air.

The Gray Claw raised its arms, revealing a disgusting smoothness on the underside of its claws—no spikes! Was he born with this deformity? Did someone remove his spikes as punishment? A Strider couldn't survive without them.

Andrés's mind raced until he noticed that the tips of the old one's claws were rounded and blunt. Now it made sense. His arms weren't malformed. They were altered. Andrés pieced together everything he'd seen on his way in —the centipedes carrying lutes, the overturned Atlas beetles, and the stage. This Gray Claw was a bard!

"We should all feel honored. That's Rimush. He'll be conducting today's battle hymn," General Cressida said.

Rimush creaked forward and stopped in the middle of the stage. He seemed lost. Could he even see? A thick yellow glaze coated his round eyes.

Malva chuckled.

Gray dots floated to the surfaces of the old mantis's compound eyes and flared into jet-black pentagrams. Malva flinched as Rimush focused his sharp gaze on her.

"Apologies," she whispered.

Steam hissed from Rimush's mandibles. He turned his attention toward the Atlas beetles. They seemed to sense his intention and turned their ample bottoms toward him.

He stepped forward and raised his claws and the two red centipedes rose to his sides like swaying cobras, clutching their lutes within spindle-thin legs.

Rimush drummed the beetles' bellies with his blunt claws. "This chant, my gentle warriors, is to protect you all on your journey to Eperu and in the fight ahead."

The centipedes strummed the lutes. Their long, segmented antennae bounced to the beat of the Gray Claw's drumming.

Rimush flared open his mandibles, revealing his human mouth. He wailed in Phantid Akkadian:

"Hear me, young warriors. Hear me well. Your Lord's protection hangs over every head and shell. He is the shield on your back, the sharpened claws on your arms, the light and savior who waits for you back in Irkalla-la-la-la . . ."

Now it was Andrés's turn to laugh. He looked at his sharp claws. What protection could the Marquis give that he wasn't already born with?

Did the Shadow Striders really believe what this bard was singing? The Marquis wasn't really with them. That psychotic mantis would never fight by their side. And he was no Lord, no God.

The Marquis was just a Strider who had clawed his way to the top. Sure, he was a rarity—a male strong and clever enough to cut through the ranks of much more capable females. But at the end of the day, he was a husk filled with green blood.

Rimush finished with a pensive tune on a pair of giant reed pipes clutched within the crooks of his smooth claws.

"Attention!" General Cressida shouted. She stomped toward the wide portal they'd be using.

Andrés stiffened in place. The general stretched out her arms and placed a travel tablet into a notch on the side of the wide arch.

"All of you know your roles. Hit the ground scurrying and I'll see you on the other side," General Cressida said, ushering her Shadow Striders though the portal. She growled as Malva approached. "Stick to the plan and don't you dare disobey my orders."

Malva smiled with her human mouth and jumped through the dark veil.

General Cressida's pupils swirled into downturned daggers as she turned her attention to Andrés.

"She'll follow orders," he assured her.

"It's your head if she doesn't," General Cressida replied.

When isn't my life on the line, Andrés thought as he jumped in. A burst of air hit his back as he felt the general step through behind him.

CHAPTER 59
OPENING MOVES

Andrés couldn't move. His body should have materialized inside the Seer's home, but he was stuck in the void between the worlds. A chorus of worried and angry voices echoed within the inky darkness.

"Where's the general?"

"Why can't we move?"

"Who the hell's in command now?"

A wave of air pushed Andrés into the world of the living. He was in the Seer's backyard again. But that didn't make any sense. The travel tablet should have put them all inside of the house.

A Shadow Strider stumbled side to side, as if drunk on aphid juice. Three of her legs were shorter than the others. Andrés saw why—the creature's feet were burned down to thin stumps.

The injured Shadow Strider's compound eye exploded, splattering webs of aqueous jelly against Andrés's face. He stood frozen as the Strider slumped forward onto the grass.

"What the hell is going on?" Andrés muttered, staring into the meaty crater where an eye used to be.

"We're being shot at!" Malva shouted from behind.

Andrés turned. The Ghost Scythe was crouched against a small tree alongside two other Shadow Striders. She pointed at the second-floor window. Andrés looked up as a puff of steam bloomed from the brightly lit opening.

A sharp pain ripped into the side of his claw and he let out a yelp.

"Idiot! Find some cover!" Malva shouted as the sound of whizzing projectiles filled the air.

Andrés jumped over Malva and flattened himself against the grass. He glanced to his sides. At least a dozen other soldiers were doing the same. "What the hell happened?"

"I don't know. They've managed to block us from entering the house. General Cressida's dead," Malva said, jutting her head toward the center of the yard where the general's corpse lay like a felled tree.

Andrés cocked his head and twitched his antennae, wondering if this was Malva's handiwork. The Ghost Scythe smiled and shook her head, as if reading his mind. She nudged the Shadow Strider next to her. "Justina here saw it happen."

"That thing in the window shot the general point blank in the head when we materialized," Justina explained, ducking at the sound of fresh nails drumming into the tree.

Serves the general right, Andrés thought, underestimating these humans. He pulled the end of the nail out of his claw with his mandibles and spat it out. It landed on the ground and sizzled as his green blood turned black.

"They've coated those missiles with the Ash of Edom. That's how they're cutting through our exoskeletons," Andrés said. "What do we do now?"

"I'm in command now," Malva said. She turned to Justina. "Take half of what's left of our strike team to the air and find a way inside the house."

The soldier nodded and darted skyward. Malva raised her voice so the other Shadow Striders pressed against the ground could hear. "And the rest of you, we're going straight in! Let's get these humans!"

The warriors scrambled forward, clawing at the ground with their spiked forelimbs. Clods of grass, dirt, and rock shot out as they sped forward. Several Striders tumbled and screamed in agony as clouds of Ash exploded beneath their bodies. More than a few didn't get up.

"Don't stop! Push forward!" Malva yelled.

Andrés slowly crawled forward. He watched as winged soldiers bounced off the house, emitting a layer of rippled light as the mantises flew into a force field over and over again.

"They've drawn Zisurrûs, the bastards," Malva said.

She was right. It was the only way to account for the travel tablet's failure. But a few Shadow Striders had made it safely to the side of the house. There was a path!

He joined Malva and what was left of their team in front of a weather-beaten wooden door. The hissing and pops from the second-floor window stopped. Now all they could hear were the moans and grunts of their wounded comrades.

Justina slammed herself against the door repeatedly

until she knocked it down. She stepped through and signaled for Malva to follow.

Andrés wrapped his claws around Malva. "This doesn't feel right!"

"What are you doing?" Malva shouted. "Let me—"

Justina screeched and tumbled backward. Her body shriveled and curled inward like a dead spider. Steam billowed from her corpse as the Ash of Edom dissolved her exoskeleton.

"The door was rigged," Andrés said, backing away from a puff of Ash floating through the entryway. After it cleared, he poked his head in slightly. The other soldier lay dead on the floor as metal fans oscillated back and forth.

Malva pushed him aside and walked in.

"Good thing I stopped you, eh? That could have been you," Andrés said. "It looks like they've improved their Ash of Edom recipe—it's potent!"

"We'll have to take it slow from here on out. Gods know what else is in here," Malva said, stepping over Justina's corpse and ordered the rest of her soldiers to follow.

Andrés scampered behind the last Shadow Strider. No sense in being the first in line. They made their way up from the basement and entered the living room. Andrés shook his head. This is where he suffered his last defeat at the hands of the Seer and the little girl.

"Careful where you step," Malva said, pointing at the dozens of black orbs that lolled on the floor. "I think there's Ash in each one."

The floorboards above their heads moaned and creaked.

Malva snarled. "Take the stairs!"

Five Shadow Striders rushed up the steps and out of view. Andrés heard a screech and the sound of wood snapping. Then silence. The soldiers tumbled back down the stairs and landed in a twisted pile of shorn wings and broken legs.

Andrés looked at Malva. The shock on her face mirrored the panic growing in his own head. How was any of this possible? The battle wasn't supposed to unfold this way.

A high-pitched roar filled the air. Only one creature could make such a sound—a scorpion.

Malva gazed at the ceiling. "There's a rogue Phantid up there."

"How many soldiers do we have left?" Andrés asked.

Malva looked around and grunted. "Ten."

Andrés made his mental calculations. Even if the Seer had a scorpion ally, they still had the numbers, but that didn't seem like much of an advantage now. "Can we take them?" he asked.

"No. Not without some help of our own." Malva fluttered her single antenna and smiled. A thunderous buzz rumbled throughout the house as thick clouds of mosquitoes, cockroaches, flies, and gnats crashed through the windows and streamed through the open basement door.

Andrés had never been happier to see tiny Crawlers in his life. The black mass pulsed through the air and made its way up the stairs.

Andrés laughed as the children shrieked.

CHAPTER 60
TRANSFORMATION

"How in the worlds did I get into this mess?" Luther asked himself.

Just a few days ago, he lived a comfortable, albeit smothering existence as the Marquis's personal secretary. Honestly, was it so bad? The work was simple and sometimes fulfilling. He would have kept that position until he died of old age or until his master decided to kill him for whatever whimsical reason crossed his deranged mind.

A Strider's screech floated up from the stairs. An invader must have set off the side door trap. The scream faded. Luther shivered—he'd yelled like that whenever the Marquis punished him.

It didn't take much to set him off, maybe a wilted petal on the Orchid Throne and the Marquis would beat Luther unconscious. On the bad days, the days Luther yelled out for mercy, the Marquis would force his way into Luther's mind and inject sordid visions and horrible nightmares. He'd shake for days after a punishment like that.

No, being stuck in Eperu was better than living another

day as a slave in the Rookery. Footsteps approached. Phantid feet—lots of Phantid feet. The odds, he now knew, weren't in his favor. Luther recognized that he might not survive the battle . . . not unless he tried something drastic.

Luther heaved in a breath of air and exhaled. "Here goes nothing."

He arched his stinger back and brought it down into his own back. The tip pierced his husk just enough to let the black tip a few inches into his body, slowly releasing the venom.

Luther raised his claws into the air and roared. His legs splayed as his body twisted and contorted into unnatural angles. An arsenal of sharp horns erupted along the length of his back and his stinger elongated into a curved stiletto with a fishhook point. Luther steadied himself on all eight legs as his claws grew longer, thicker, and sharper.

He snapped his claws shut and winced as the sound echoed through the hallway. The footsteps he heard earlier turned into a running march up the stairs.

Suddenly, a group of Shadow Striders were on his back, trying their best to slice through his exoskeleton. And, in a flash, Luther was looking down the stairs at the soldiers' twitching corpses.

"How in the worlds did I do that?" Luther asked.

His self-imposed transformation helped him defeat some of the best Shadow Striders in Irkalla, but his powers wouldn't last long. He could already feel the spikes on his body shrinking. And he couldn't risk another injection. His own venom would probably kill him next time.

Luther had to make a move, but just as he decided what to do a torrent of insects flowed up the stairs, blocking his vision.

CHAPTER 61
FUBAR

Edgar yanked clumps of writhing cockroaches from his face and crushed them within clenched fists, but the living muck pooled back onto his skin again and again. Streaks of burgundy bloomed on his cheeks as his fingers raked through a fresh layer of roaches.

The buzzsaw hum reverberating in the air exploded into a monstrous roar as more insects rammed their way into the bedroom. Edgar yelled as a bolt of hot pain buried into the back of his neck. He smacked a palm over his nape, finding the source of his misery—a six-inch long centipede.

"Oh, God! It's stuck!" Edgar yelled, tugging at the creature as it buried its pincers even deeper. Edgar's stomach turned. He hoped someone would come over and pull it off, but his mom, Clara, and Aunt Ginnie were rolling on the floor trying to crush the bugs coating their bodies, and Opa Chuck fluttered through the air.

Only Sol remained calm. He stood in the center of the room as the mass of insects streamed around his body.

"This is my fault," he shouted. "I should have considered they'd use this tactic."

"What do we do?" Edgar asked.

Sol reached into his coat pocket and threw out a handful of Ash of Edom in a wide arc. The flying insects caught in the cloud sizzled and dropped to the ground. The rest of the swarm retreated out the window or under the door.

The professor stepped behind Edgar and yanked the centipede out from his neck. It flailed in his fist like an out-of-control fire hose. He threw the creature on the floor and stomped it to mush.

"Get these things off of me!" Aunt Ginnie yelled. Her plea was followed by the sound of vomit spluttering on the floor. Clara and Margaret moaned; trickles of vomit flowed down their mouths, collecting gnats and mosquitoes in their viscous flow. A halo of black flies hummed around their lolling heads.

Edgar swatted the remaining bugs from his mother with his hands. Sol did the same with a towel for Aunt Ginnie and Clara.

"If we get out of this alive, I'm never touching another bug in my life," Clara said, wiping her face with the back of her hand.

Edgar hugged Clara. "Don't worry. We're getting out of this." He looked back at Sol. "How are we getting out of this?"

"Well," he said. "We can't stay here anymore. All the Zisurrûs we drew here were erased during this ruckus. There's nothing stopping the Striders from coming into this room. Let's grab the spears and head up to the attic with Sharur."

Edgar rolled his eyes. "Spears? These are broomsticks, Sol!" He picked up the shortest of the bunch and gestured at its jagged tip. "Splintered broomsticks with barely any points!"

"Edgar! It's all we have left to defend ourselves with," Margaret said, handing the remaining arsenal out to Aunt Ginnie and Clara.

Edgar's head drooped to his chest. She was right, but it wasn't fair. Sol's battle plan should have gone smoother than this. The thin stick in his hand didn't fill him with confidence even if it was covered in a thick coat of Ash paste. And the sudden appearance of the insect swarms made Edgar feel vulnerable. Mortal is what Clara would say. He didn't want to sound like a coward or a quitter, but the words spilled out anyway.

"We're losing now, aren't we?" Edgar asked.

Sol placed a hand on his shoulder. "It's ok, Edgar. We can do this. We still have Luther and Sharur." Sol fiddled with the top of his walking cane. The gold monkey head turned with a click and slid out, revealing a razor-sharp sword. "Besides, I still have tricks up my sleeve."

Edgar smiled. "Ok. You said we should make our way up to the attic if anything went wrong, right?"

"That's right. Lead the way, m'boy."

Edgar marched to the door and pressed his ear against the wood. He could still hear the hum of other insect swarms in the house and Luther thumping around on the landing. He opened a gap and spied the scorpion waving his claws in the air and struggling against the clouds of insects. His blue body looked like it was coated in black and brown paint.

"We should go," Sol said.

Edgar threw the door open and ushered everyone out. He turned and ran up to the attic as quickly as he could and looked back to check on Luther one more time. His stinger waved in the air, smashing into the walls and squirting venom in all directions.

"Good luck, big guy," Edgar said and rushed into his bedroom.

He slammed the door shut and took a step back.

He could still hear Luther's muffled voice through the door, followed by a Strider's yell. Edgar winced as a series of sharp cracks echoed out—as if someone was chopping at an oak tree with a baseball bat.

Edgar looked back to Sol. "Do you think Luther's ok?"

The professor shook his head and pulled Edgar back from the door.

CHAPTER 62
DUELING PHANTIDS

Andrés swatted at the thick, thrumming clouds of insects whirling around his body. The darkness parted briefly as the wooden steps groaned under his weight. He swiped again.

"Careful!" Malva hissed, as his claw scraped the end of her rump.

He caught a brief glimpse of her pale body before she was again enveloped by the millions of black bugs swirling in the air. The same swarms Malva called upon to confuse the Seer and his allies were now hindering their progress up the stairs.

Andrés winced as one of the Shadow Striders following him sliced at the back of his leg. Even the Rookery's best were having a hard time. *A raging Irkallan dust storm,* Andrés thought, *would be preferable to enduring another second inside this living squall.* At least sand particles didn't try to eat the meat between his jointed segments.

"Malva, this is ridiculous!" Andrés shouted. "It's time to call the swarm off."

The humming dissipated and the murkiness thinned. Malva stood at the top of the staircase, frozen. *Why wasn't she moving?* Andrés took a few steps up and saw the blurred outline of an enormous scorpion blocking the way to the Seer's room.

"This doesn't make any sense." Andrés twitched his head back and forth, shaking off a layer of stubborn flies and gnats. "It couldn't be."

His mind refused to believe he was looking at Luther—the Marquis's personal secretary. But the Rookery's glorified royal servant was larger now, much larger. His gnarled claws were three times their normal size, a forest of long barbs dotted his back, and his segmented armored plates had thickened, giving him a medieval appearance.

"The crazy bastard self-injected," Malva said.

"Yes! I should have done this years ago!" Luther growled. Foamy spittle dripped from his human mouth. He arched his stinger toward Malva and Andrés. The sharp point seemed to grow longer as it bobbed in the air. "The same venom that kills, gives me a jolt of power."

But not for long, Andrés thought. *Not for long.* Luther's newfound form would only last a few minutes, but there was no way to tell if he was at the start of his transformation or the tail end. It didn't matter—they had to get through him now.

But before they could make a move, Luther charged forward, ramming into Malva. She locked onto Luther's shell and tumbled backward, taking Andrés and the Shadow Strider behind him along for the ride. They tumbled down the stairs, wrapped in a ball of spiny appendages.

Luther twisted free on the bottom floor and faced the two mantises.

Andrés snarled and unfurled his clawed forearms while Malva jumped, twisting her body upside down and clamping her legs onto the ceiling.

"This Crawler is for me and Andrés to deal with!" Malva yelled, addressing the remaining Shadow Striders. The dark warriors skulked backward and formed a semi-circle around the combatants.

Luther took a few steps toward Andrés and retreated. The blue scorpion's beady eyes rolled in their hard sockets, focusing on an inverted Malva crawling toward him from the ceiling. Luther's tail tensed and slowly angled its tip at the Ghost Scythe's head.

Andrés rushed at Luther's right flank, confident he'd avoid claw and stinger. He was wrong. Very wrong. Luther clasped Andrés's front leg with one pincer and clamped around Malva's chest with the other. Andrés tried to back away, but he was trapped.

Luther flared his arms out, ripping Andrés's leg off and wrenching Malva from the ceiling in one fluid motion. Andrés tried standing, but toppled to his side with a wet thud as he tried to lean on the missing limb. Blood gushed from his wound, making the ground impossible to stand on. All he could do was look on as Luther squeezed Malva. She screeched as long cracks raced across her thorax.

The Shadow Striders pounced.

They wrapped themselves around Luther's throbbing tail and claws, giving one of the Shadow Striders a chance to pry Malva out. As the Ghost Scythe wriggled away,

Luther's stinger plunged into the Strider who saved Malva with a squelch, pinning her to the wall.

Malva sliced off the bulbous end of Luther's stinger with a downward stroke and collapsed. Luther roared and scurried backward as silver venom squirted from the wound. The Shadow Striders swarmed the scorpion, slashing at the armored spikes on his back until they were harmless nubs while Andrés sat there and oozed from his leg. They plunged their claws deep into Luther's shell. Geysers of blue blood gushed from Luther's injuries.

The scorpion managed to grab one of the Striders on his back and snap it in half before his legs gave out.

Andrés wobbled forward. "My Gods, Luther. I didn't expect that kind of fight from the Marquis's secretary."

Blood sputtered from Luther's mouths. "Come closer."

Andrés sneered and lowered himself. "What? You have some last words? Something to put me in my place?"

Luther smacked Andrés's claw, striking the same wound Edgar had left behind, creating a deeper crater.

"Limp claw," Luther gurgled. He widened what was left of his mouth into a broken smile and died.

CHAPTER 63
THE ALAMO

Sol placed a palm on the attic door.

The battle between Luther and the Striders reverberated against the thin wood. Sol covered his ears as a barrage of squeals, scrapes, and screeches pierced the air.

The house grew quiet.

Perhaps Luther accomplished the impossible and forced the Striders into a retreat. It wasn't such a crazy thought, but then Malva laughed.

Sol's head drooped to his chest.

"Luther's gone, isn't he?" Sharur asked.

"I'm afraid so."

One of Sol's oldest friends in all the worlds was gone and it was his fault. Luther had only come up because he badgered him into bringing Ginnie back. He got what he wanted, but at a terrible cost.

Sol clutched his cane until his hands turned white. All he wanted to do was skulk into a corner and beat his head against the wall, but there wasn't time for self-loathing. He needed to steady his nerves and rile up his own ragtag team—what was left of them—for the fight coming their way.

Sol took a deep breath and turned to face Sharur, Edgar, Clara, Ginnie, Margaret, and Opa Chuck. "They'll be coming up now. Malva, Andrés, and whatever's left of the Shadow Striders. We have to make our stand here." Sol tapped his cane on the floor. "Sharur, front and center please."

The staff floated over and faced the door.

"I'll need you to crush whatever tries to come through this door. Please, don't hold back. Do your worst." Sol pointed to the opposite side of the room. "There's an extra Zisurrû there, big enough for Edgar and Charles to stand in—"

Edgar shook his head. "No, no way. I want to fight!"

Sol placed a hand on his shoulder. "You are your grandfather's last line of defense. The circle will shield you from their attacks, but if they get through . . ." Sol glanced at the broomstick clutched in the boy's hands. "Drive that into their guts, and don't forget that you can hurt these creatures with your bare hands too."

Opa Chuck fluttered over Edgar's shoulder. "We'll be ok. This grandson of mine is a real fighter, aren't you?"

Edgar smiled weakly.

"Good. The rest of us will stand in front of the Zisurrû with our spears pointing forward like a good old-fashioned Greek phalanx," Sol said, gently shepherding the group into position with his cane.

The stairs creaked.

Sol turned just in time to see the door explode. The blast knocked everyone, even Edgar and Opa Chuck, backward. A high-pitched whine filled Sol's ears. He rolled off his back and sat up. The door was gone. He glanced around the room. Everyone lay flat on the floor and Charles's head was wedged halfway into the wall. All Sol could see was the smooth porcelain base of the old ghost's neck. Sharur was nowhere to be seen.

Nothing's stopping them now, Sol thought. Then, as if reading his mind, a dark, four-legged figure emerged from the jagged hole where the door used to stand. A Shadow Strider crawled forward and examined Sol with her bulbous obsidian eyes. Her antennae whipped the air as more of the creatures flooded the room.

The largest leaped toward Sol with flared wings and outstretched claws, her red mandibles clattered open and closed. All Sol could do was raise his hands and hope for a quick death. But the moment of impact never came.

The Strider hovered in the air, screaming at the sight of Sharur's head erupting from her chest. The staff corkscrewed out, pulling flaps of steaming viscera and chunks of exoskeleton through the creature's spasming body until she collapsed near Sol's feet.

Sharur stood upright and winked at Sol before zooming across the room and smashing through the remaining soldiers. Sheets of green blood splattered against the walls and onto Edgar, Clara, Ginnie, and Margaret. They awoke with a start, screaming at the sight of the massacre.

The Storm Striders' mangled corpses, severed claws, and legs twitched on the floor.

Edgar stood and wiped mantis blood from his face. "Is that it? Did we win?" He hobbled around the room, staring at the Phantid corpses. "Where's Malva? Where's Andrés?"

"They're probably downstairs. I'll go check. Everyone stay here," Sharur said, floating toward the exit. Just as he reached the threshold, a bright green claw shot through the floorboards and took hold of the staff's pommel.

Malva sped into the room and grasped Sharur's head in the crook of her pale, violet claws. Steam bellowed out of Sharur's nostrils as he tried to break free. Malva hissed, dug her legs onto the floor, and twisted Sharur's head.

"Someone help him!" Ginnie shouted.

Edgar rushed forward, but Sol held him back. It was too dangerous. The boy struggled in Sol's grasp as Sharur rose into the air, pulling up Malva and Andrés, who remained clamped on his pommel below the splintered floorboards. Malva's head crunched against the attic's angled ceiling. Blood dribbled from the cracks in her chest and black goo oozed from her mandibles and human lips.

Sharur opened his mouth. A sharp note blasted like a horn and the staff shot straight through the ceiling, carrying Malva and Andrés into the sky. Sol looked through the jagged hole and watched as they flew skyward and then fell back toward the ground.

Sol fell to his knees as strange vibrations rattled the house.

"Was that an earthquake?" Margaret asked, pulling Sol to his feet.

"No, I think those are our reinforcements. Come on, we need to get out of here," Sol said.

CHAPTER 64
THANATOPSIS

Edgar braced one hand against the wall and clutched Opa Chuck's neck with the other. He counted to three and pulled. Sweat dripped from Edgar's forehead as his muscles strained to pull Opa free from the plaster, but it was no use.

"Ugh! He's really stuck in there." Edgar stepped back and wiped away a tiny stream of blood dribbling from his nose. His lungs burned, his head ached, and his guts hurt, especially his stomach. If he felt this bad, he wondered if the explosion had done more than just knock Opa unconscious. *Could he die again?*

Sol caught his eye and saw his worried expression. "That wasn't an ordinary blast. The Shadow Striders used their black pneuma to break through. The concussive force ripped through the living and the dead. That's why your grandfather's still out like a light."

"When will he wake up?" Edgar asked.

"No idea, but we shouldn't stay here a minute longer."

Sol glanced at Clara. "Maybe the two of you can twist him out?"

It was worth a shot, Edgar thought. *Clara could use the Catch.* He stepped aside and adjusted his grip to give her hand enough space on Opa's neck to clamp onto. They yanked and twisted. At first, nothing happened, but then Opa's head squeaked a few inches out from the plaster.

"Almost there, Edgar," Clara said. She threw her head back. "Come on, all at once now!"

Edgar closed his eyes and pulled as hard as he could. Clara growled and Edgar joined in with a long, "Gaaaah!"

With a champagne-cork-pop, Opa Chuck came loose. Everyone cheered as he spun around the room. Edgar jumped and caught his grandfather mid-flight. He pressed Opa close to his chest and then raised him up. He was awake, but there was a strange, far-off look in his eyes.

"Opa, are you ok?"

"I-I remember."

Edgar raised an eyebrow. "Remember what?"

"How I died. I remember how I died," Opa whispered.

Everyone, except Sol, shuffled closer. The professor rolled his eyes. "Listen, we don't have time for this. Andrés and Malva could be—"

Opa zoomed out of Edgar's grasp and toward Sol, stopping a hair's breadth from his nose. "I said, I remember!"

Sol raised his palms. "Ok, ok. Go on, sir."

Edgar couldn't believe his ears! Opa was going to finish his story—the story! He sat and listened to his grandfather. He knew most of the details by heart, but then Opa veered off.

"It was an old boiler. Christ, a boiler explosion! I wasn't

even supposed to be there. I'd been retired from the station for about a year, but I went to most of the calls, you know? I'd already been to one apartment fire earlier that day, as Edgar knows."

"No, not all of us know about this. I don't know," Margaret said. "Where in the world did this all happen?"

"Back in St. Louis."

"What the hell! Missouri?"

"Yes, yes, but—wait, is that what you're focused on? I've been trying to remember how I kicked the can for the past eleven years and now that I've got the answer, you're stuck on—"

"Well, I didn't know it was a mystery!" Margaret said.

"Mom, please let him finish. We've been trying to figure this out since I was a little kid," Edgar said. "Opa, focus! You're so close."

"Whatever," Margaret mumbled.

"Right, so like I was saying—St. Louis—it was a cardboard box company. A nightshift worker had called in a gas leak. Pretty standard stuff. I heard the alert go out on the scanner, jumped in the car, and radioed in that I'd meet the boys there."

This was it! The moment Opa would normally fall asleep. Edgar's stomach curdled as Opa lowered his gaze. *Oh, no. He's going out. He's going to fall asleep.*

Opa's eyes fluttered back open. "I wasn't supposed to even be there. But, God, I loved the job, that life, and especially my brothers. It's not like I had anyone at home to keep me there. So, I went. I didn't even make it out of the car."

"What do you mean?" Edgar asked.

"Boom!" Opa shouted. "The boiler exploded as I pulled

into the parking lot. A van-sized chunk of metal crashed on top of my head."

"You mean, your car," Margaret said.

Opa Chuck laughed. "It was a convertible."

Edgar didn't know how to react. They had their answer, and it seemed so obvious now. *Of course Opa Chuck died on the job! How else could it have happened?* Edgar frowned. He was disappointed with the truth. He thought back to his two favorite childhood suspects: a sword-wielding pirate and a runaway circular saw from a timber yard.

Edgar laughed.

"Isn't that crazy?" Opa Chuck asked.

"It's nuts!" Edgar said. "But how did you end up as a ghost without a body?"

Sol cleared his throat. "I can answer that. A traumatic death like that interrupts the soul's journey forward," Sol said. "One becomes stuck between the worlds."

"Right, but how did I end up here in New York, in this house, with just a head?" Opa Chuck asked.

"When exactly was the accident?" Sol asked.

"I'd guess almost twelve years ago," Opa Chuck said.

"A double tether." Sol paced the room and stroked his beard. He turned to face Charles. "At the moment of death, your spirit focused on your most important connection to this world—Margaret."

"Now, it takes a lot of energy to cross time and space like that. That's why when you appeared here, it was just your head. Honestly, at that point you should have dissolved back into the land of the dead, but if the timing is what you say it is, then it was Edgar, in Margaret's womb, that anchored you home."

"Wait, what? How did I do that?"

"Edgar, at the moment of conception, you were gifted the abilities of a Seer," Sol said. "You had these powers even as a wee little thing in your mother's belly. Your underdeveloped energy kept Charles trapped between the worlds like a magnet."

"So, it's my fault. It's my fault that—"

"No, not at all," Sol said. "It's just a bit of exotic nature at play."

"And I wouldn't have had it any other way." Opa Chuck bobbed over to Margaret and shepherded her close to Edgar. "The past few years with the both of you have been the best in my life. I just wish that—"

The floorboards and walls rumbled again. The lights flickered on and off.

"Well, this has all been very lovely, but we still need to get the hell out of this house," Sol said. "We don't want to be trapped up here if Malva and Andrés survived."

CHAPTER 65
BUTCHER'S BILL

Edgar rushed down the stairs, one hand on the railing and the other braced the wall, balancing himself as the house rocked from side to side. The wood frame behind the plaster walls moaned. Halfway down from the attic, he heard his name whispered, as if squeezed from air. The voice sounded just like Lugal.

Edgar slowed down and pressed his ear against the wall. Clara slammed into his back as Aunt Ginnie, Sol, and his mom weaved around and thundered down the stairs. Even Opa Chuck zipped past.

"What are you doing?" Clara smacked his shoulder. "We need to get out of here!"

"Sorry, but did you just hear that?"

"Hear what? The house collapsing? Yeah!"

An overhead light exploded, showering the two with shards of glass and electric sparks. A photo from his parents' wedding flashed in Edgar's mind—his mother and father covering their heads as a barrage of white rice peppered their heads. *Why am I thinking about that right now?*

Clara pushed him forward. "Let's go, Edgar!"

Edgar obliged and skipped the last few steps. The second-floor landing looked like a war zone. The carpet was shredded to bits and the walls were smeared with streaks of green and blue. He didn't want to think about whose blood it belonged to. He hardly knew Luther, but he hoped that somehow he was still ok.

Someone cried downstairs.

"That sounds like my aunt," Clara said.

"Or my mom," Edgar said, starting down the final set of stairs.

He stopped a few steps from the bottom of the stairs, which was blocked by what looked like a heap of black garbage bags. It took his eyes a moment to recognize the shapes for what they really were—dead Shadow Striders. The last thing he wanted to do was crawl over their lifeless shells, so he jumped over what was left of the wood railing. Clara followed his lead and landed by his side.

More Strider corpses littered the ground floor, severed wings, shards of pale purple exoskeleton, and a single, green leg. One of the creatures, slumped against the wall, was cut down the middle, revealing a perfect cross section. The carnage was brutal. Edgar picked up a shard of exoskeleton—it was at least three inches thick!

How, Edgar wondered, *would they ever have fought them off without Luther and Sharur?* He shook his head. *No, their sharpened sticks wouldn't have lasted a minute.*

His mother rushed over and knocked the shard out of his hand. "You two have to help me. Ginevra and Sol are a mess."

"What happened? Are they ok?"

"They're fine, but they won't stop crying." Margaret gestured toward the hallway. Just a few feet away, Sol and Aunt Ginnie kneeled beside the remains of Luther.

Two lifeless Shadow Striders lay draped over the scorpion's pale blue shell like funerary shrouds. Steam billowed from fleshy craters dug into Luther's back, deep gashes zigzagged along his abdomen, and threads of pale meat splayed out from the ends of broken legs. Worst of all was his human face—frozen in a bloody sneer.

Sol buried his face in his hands and wept. Aunt Ginnie stood and pulled off the top half of a dead Shadow Strider from Luther's back. The creature landed with a hollow thud.

She looked at Edgar. "He saved me, you know. Luther and Sharur got me out of that awful place and brought me back home." Aunt Ginnie's shoes squelched in the pool of cerulean blood spread across the floor. "He was so brave."

"I'm so sorry," Edgar said.

What else could he say? His mother, Clara, and Opa Chuck approached. They seemed just as speechless as he was.

"Luther saved us all." Sol wiped the tears from his face with the back of his hand.

"I get that you have lost someone, but we need to get a move on and think about what to do next," Margaret said.

"Mom's right. We should get as far away as—"

Windows shattered as the house rocked back and forth again.

The tremor faded quickly, replaced by the sound of heavy footsteps. No, something heavier than human footsteps.

Malva's raspy voice echoed through the house, "Edgar, honey, won't you join us in the living room again? I have something to show you."

CHAPTER 66
REVELATIONS

Edgar stopped at the edge of the hallway and glanced back to check on his companions. *Why was it always the living room?*

It was one of the most relaxing spaces in the house, but now every inch of the family room reminded him of yesterday's horrors—Andrés squeezing Opa between spiked forelimbs, Malva screaming as the Ash of Edom burned her face, Aunt Ginnie disappearing, and his painful trip to Kur, the underworld.

All of that happened between those four walls, and it was the last place he wanted to go, but he had no choice. They had to face Malva and Andrés.

"We're with you, Edgar," Sol said. "I have my cane and we all have some Ash in our pockets."

Clara patted her cargo pants and grinned. "Lots of pockets."

Margaret flattened herself against the wall. She stared at the ceiling. "God, why can't we just run away?"

Aunt Ginnie clutched one of the last Ash-tipped broomsticks. "They'll just run us down. You saw how fast those dark mantises were, right?"

"We barely survived that!" Margaret threw her hands up.

"Calm down, Mrs. Tooms. All we have to do is stall them until Sharur comes back or the Myrmidon arrive," Sol said. "Let's keep moving."

Edgar led the group toward the living room. He could see Malva looming ahead with her long, thin back turned toward them. Andrés squatted to the right of her. Thick clumps of dark goo congealed around a hole where one of his legs should have been. He wobbled at Malva's side.

"We're here," Edgar said. "What do you want?"

The Ghost Scythe turned. The dark pupils in her upturned almond-shaped eyes bounced back and forth. The plating surrounding her human mouth hung like broken shingles after a storm. A large, pale square peeled away from her chin and fell off.

Edgar thought they could take her and Andrés on. They seemed weak, broken. But then his eyes caught sight of a package wrapped in linen clenched in the crook of Malva's claw. She pressed the object against her cracked chest where thick green blood oozed from her wounds, staining the cloth. Edgar could see the faint outline of a large head bleeding through the bloody cloth.

Malva loosened her grip and let the contents roll out. Sharur's head landed with a thump at her feet. His golden features smudged beyond recognition.

Edgar's heart sank. He heard Aunt Ginnie gasp.

Malva flicked open her spiked forelimbs. "I'm sorry.

Was the Smasher of Thousands supposed to be your ultimate weapon?"

"You bastards!" Opa Chuck shouted, rising in the air.

"Hello, old man," Andrés said, hobbling toward Opa. He rubbed his claws together. "I believe this is where we first met. It's time I took you back to the Rookery and let Malva here eviscerate your grandson and his little friends."

Sol stepped between Andrés and Opa Chuck. "No! This ends here."

Malva laughed and jabbed Andrés with the dull side of her claw. "Look, a fighter."

Andrés rose on three spindly legs. "Old man, you'd better step aside or—"

Before the green mantis could finish his sentence, Sol whipped out his sword from his cane and sliced Andrés with an upward stroke. The metal blade clanged against the creature's hard armor. Andrés stumbled backward and glanced down at his chest. Beads of green blood bubbled from a thin gash.

Andrés snarled, sinking the curved edge of his right claw into Sol's head. A spray of blood hissed from the wound, coating everyone nearby in a thin sheen of red. Sol's cane fell out of his trembling, outstretched palm. Aunt Ginnie screamed.

"There! How's that feel? Not so good, eh?" Andrés said, pressing deeper into Sol's skull. The beady pupils in Andrés's eyes swirled into massive starbursts as the professor's hands suddenly grasped his claw.

Edgar couldn't believe what he was seeing. The professor was alive, and he was fighting back!

"Andrés! What's happening?" Malva shrieked. She scrambled to her partner's side. "Oh, Gods! Let go. Let go now!"

"I-I'm trying," Andrés said, struggling to free his forelimb from Sol's skull.

Sol took a step back. Then another. Andrés clamped his feet onto the carpet, but the professor marched backward. Edgar could now see what had shocked the Striders—Sol's yellow eyes shone through cracked sunglasses while black porridge oozed between his clenched teeth.

The professor smiled. "This feels just fine, brother. But we haven't gone far enough, have we?"

Sol jerked the claw in his skull down, forcing it to slice through the length of his entire body. The momentum lodged Andrés's claw tip deep into the floor.

Sol's body peeled apart and flopped on the carpet. Everyone stared at his spine, at the thick, pale worm wrapped around what was left of his vertebrae. It squirmed, but how? That's when Edgar saw its face—it was a Strider! A baby of some kind and . . . growing.

The grub-like creature flopped over what was left of Sol's body and fattened, tripling in size. Its insides swelled with dark fluid and a network of blue and green veins raced across its taut surface before snapping apart, splashing viscous goo around the room.

Edgar wiped the mess from his face and rubbed his eyes. Right where Sol had stood loomed another gigantic mantis. The creature's thick husk gleamed like polished bronze, its four legs, spiked arms, and underside were painted a splotchy mess of muddy green and sky blue, and elaborate rows of raised dots ran along the seams of its shell like rivets. Steam hissed from its chittering mandibles.

Andrés screeched as the enormous mantis raised a claw, hovering the sickle-shaped blade over him, sped it down, and lopped Andrés's head clean off.

CHAPTER 67

HEADHUNTERS

Edgar flattened himself against the floor as chunks of furniture, glass, and plaster flew through the air. The moment Andrés's head hit the floor, Malva started destroying the living room, slashing at the furniture and smashing windows. Now she seemed hell-bent on breaking down the walls. *Was Andrés that important to her?* Edgar wondered if maybe the green mantis was her mate.

His mother cursed as the overhead fan rocked out of the ceiling and crashed to the floor. Edgar rolled over to his side and glanced back. Aunt Ginnie, Clara, and his mother were on the ground too. Opa Chuck peeked through the carpet with the top half of his head. Clara jutted her chin toward the bronze giant just a few feet in front of Edgar.

The enormous bronze mantis stood still, taking the brunt of the debris Malva hurtled their way. Most of the pieces bounced off after smacking its hard shell, but some of it slapped against what sounded like skin. Edgar stared at the creature. He could see the sides and underside of its torpedo-shaped belly were thick, but nothing like the plated top—the texture was more like tough leather. It looked vulnerable.

Malva roared.

The new Strider mirrored Malva's position, placing itself in front of her. *Was it protecting them?* Edgar's mind raced. *Was that thing always inside of Sol like some kind of parasite? Or was this the professor's true form?*

He didn't have time to process all the questions he had. Malva stared directly at him now. What was left of her face plates shut. She scuttled forward and leaped into the air. The bronze mantis threw itself against her body and they crashed onto the floor.

Edgar rolled back to safety with the rest of the group and watched as the two creatures wrapped their claws and gangly legs around each other. Even their long abdomens wriggled and wrestled. Locked in a tight embrace, their heads twisted and jerked in all directions as each tried to snap into the other's neck stalk with their thick mandibles. Malva knocked the larger mantis off with her four legs and scuttled into the far corner of the room.

"Who in the worlds are you?" Malva asked, shaking her head.

"Do they not teach history in the Rookery anymore? You don't recognize Ugallu?"

Edgar couldn't see his protector's face, but he recognized the voice. It was Sol!

"The traitor? But that's impossible. You'd have to be—"

"Old? Yes, I am very, very old. A Gray Claw. The last of the Ancient Ones, my dear," Sol said.

"I'll kill you for what you did to Andrés," Malva said.

The ground trembled. A horrible screech echoed

throughout the house as if God had dragged their finger-nails across the sky. Edgar clapped his hands over his ears.

Malva squatted, tucking in her arms and legs. She looked terrified.

"That's not going to happen, Malva," Ugallu said, crawling backward.

Malva raised her claws. "Why not?"

"Because we opened the gates to Kur." Sol's antennae fluttered. "The Myrmidon are coming. I can smell them."

"You're lying!" Malva took a step forward just as a sinkhole opened beneath her feet. Her body sank into the gaping crater. As she tried to claw her way out, something pulled her into the pit. The tips of her claws carved jagged grooves into the carpet, pulling up the wood underneath, as she slipped further in.

"No! No! Get off me!" She screamed as dozens of mastiff-sized ants swarmed out of the hole and clamped onto her arms, claws, and legs with their serrated mandibles. Unlike the giant Myrmidon Edgar met in Kur, these smaller ants had dozens of beady eyes dotting their wedged heads.

Malva exhaled plumes of black smoke. The wisps formed themselves into daggers, turned in the air, and rained down on the ants. The sharpened pneuma evapo-rated into harmless mist as they hit their targets. Malva screamed as more ants pinned her down, biting her back and belly.

Edgar winced as the Myrmidon's thick, hairy jaws snapped through Malva's hard outer shell. Her body jerked back and forth as the ants nuzzled deeper, revealing green blood and stringy white meat from her wounds.

Malva's pupils swirled into downturned crescents. "Mercy. Please, mercy!"

It was the last thing she said.

Black froth spurted from Malva's mouths as the ants twisted off her limbs. The Ghost Scythe's body slumped forward, the top half resting over the edge of the crater.

The largest of the strange new ants crawled over Malva's back and clamped down on her neck stalk, slicing through the thick armor. Malva's head rolled onto the carpet just as other Headhunter ants dragged her limp body into the pit and out of sight.

The victorious ant gently pinched the Ghost Scythe's severed head between its jaws and turned to face its compatriots. They angled their heads left and right, chittering wildly while stomping their feet.

The house rocked back and forth as another crater opened, swallowing what was left of the TV stand and couch. The ants skittered around the newly formed edge and bowed their bulbous heads as Lugal, the Ant King, crawled out from the hole. He was smaller than Edgar remembered, now the size of the couch that just disappeared.

Edgar held out his arms and slowly walked backward, shepherding his family out of the room. He stood at the threshold as Lugal crawled forward.

"It's nice to see you again, young man," Lugal said as a few of the smaller ants crawled playfully around his thorny body. He gently pinched one by its neck and set it down. It skittered away. "I see you've met some of my Headhunters. We've been breeding them down in Kur for a very long time now. They're smaller, faster, and even more ruthless than my soldier ants. They're also immune to Strider pneuma."

"We saw them in action. They killed Malva," Edgar said.

"Is that who that was?" Lugal said. He turned his gaze toward Andrés's head by the wall. "My creations made short work of that one too. It seems that all of your problems have disappeared."

Edgar stared at Sol in the far corner of the room. He was cleaning his antennae between his mandibles. Lugal turned. "Ah, yes. The Ancient One. The traitor—Ugallu."

The bronze mantis's mandibles and mouth plates peeled back. The professor's human mouth emerged from the darkness. "I prefer Sol, if you don't mind."

"I see you've abandoned your camouflage," Lugal said.

"I had to protect my friends." Sol jutted his chins toward Edgar and his family. Opa Chuck floated over Edgar's shoulder.

The Ant King's antennae stiffened. Their blunt tips tracked Opa's movement, bouncing up and down.

"Edgar, your grandfather looks delicious," Lugal said.

Edgar waved his hands in the air. "No! Please, please leave him alone!"

"Our people haven't fed properly in centuries. I haven't fed in centuries . . ."

"You promised!"

"I did no such thing. I warned you that all souls are fair game," Lugal said as his Headhunters stalked forward.

Their black eyes jiggled with excitement; webs of sticky saliva dripped from glossy mandibles, and the fine red hairs dotting their hard outer shells thickened into sharp thorns. This was the moment Edgar feared the most. Lugal had warned him. Threatened him. He saw how quickly these Headhunters killed Malva and knew that they didn't stand a chance. Their only hope was Sol.

Edgar looked toward the transformed professor. He had already spread his translucent wings and raised his claws. His mandibles snapped back, hiding his human face. The movement reminded Edgar of a medieval knight sliding a visor in place. Sol crouched. His thin legs bowed, primed to launch forward.

Lugal glared at Sol and seemed to be sizing him up. The Ant King shook his head and stomped his feet. "Heel!"

The Headhunters squatted on their egg-shaped abdomens. They twisted their heads back like puppies.

"Very good, very good," Lugal said, fluttering his antennae. In response, the smaller Myrmidon crawled back into the crater. "Forgive my behavior. Our behavior. It's hard to control, but I assure you, you have nothing to fear from us, young man. I am familiar with the ordeal you and your friends have gone through."

Edgar exhaled. *Thank God*, he thought.

"You all deserve a reprieve, at least for a few days," Lugal said. The Ant King crawled to face Sol. "I'd ask Sol here to take your grandfather somewhere safer. There are worlds where he can live without fear of Phantids. Better yet, he could move forward into the next phase of his existence."

Sol lowered his arms and shook his head. "I'd love to help him travel, but we don't have a tablet anymore." Sol pointed a claw toward Opa. "And Charles there doesn't seem ready to pass."

"I see. Well, it would be bad form if I didn't help,

seeing as how you two freed us from Kur." Lugal rubbed his antennae together. The crater rumbled and a black ant the size of a small dog skittered out from the rubble. The little ant dropped two clay slabs at Sol's clawed feet.

"Ah! It's so cute!" Clara said.

"That is my gift to you, Ugallu," the Ant King said.

Sol bowed. "Thank you. I'll use one to take Mr. Tooms somewhere . . . safer."

"I see . . . he's in good claws then," Lugal said, turning back to face Edgar. "You have my thanks, young human."

"Wait, where are you going now?" Edgar asked.

"We have a kingdom to topple. The Marquis isn't going to let go of the Rookery without a fight." Lugal stomped toward the crater's edge and paused. "Ugallu, wherever you go, I'd suggest you stay clear of Irkalla until we've finished with it."

The Ant King crawled back into the hole and disappeared in a cloud of thick, black smoke. The vapor filled in the crater, condensed, and hardened into smooth asphalt. Edgar stepped into the living room followed by Clara, Aunt Ginnie, his mother, and Opa Chuck.

Edgar dropped to his knees. "It's over."

CHAPTER 68
SURVIVORS

Ginnie stepped into the living room unsure of what she would say to the creature she once knew as Sol Balam. He loomed in the far corner, transformed from a sprightly elderly professor into a ten-foot-tall praying mantis with half a human face.

She'd fallen in love with that face years ago. Ginnie realized that she'd probably never see Sol's visage in full ever again. The only familiar features left within that gaping insect maw were his nose, cheeks, mouth, and chin. What was it that Luther had called it? A pānu?

Whatever it was called, it was a perfect re-creation, reproducing Sol's complexion, wrinkles, laugh lines, and even his beard and mustache.

"I'm sure you have questions," Sol asked, snapping Ginnie out of her daze.

She nodded. There was so much to say, but the words wouldn't come out. All she could do was stare. She shuddered as dark rectangular pupils swam in and out of focus within the domes of his honey-colored eyes.

Sol lowered his triangular head, drooping his long antennae. "I know that I look like a monster to you. And I'm so—"

All she wanted to do was hug him now. She rushed forward and tripped as her feet sunk within the still steaming asphalt Lugal had left behind. Sol caught her with the smooth parts of his claws.

"Thank you," Ginnie said, regaining her balance. She stepped back and raised her hand. Sol lowered his head and nuzzled her palm, purring like a cat—a giant cat wearing a steel helmet—and Ginnie felt the vibrations through his thick, cold shell.

"I don't think you're a monster," she said. "You'll always be my Sol."

"I thought you'd be mad."

"I am. Just a little. You did lie to me about who you really are." Ginnie pulled her hand back. "Sol, is this really you?"

"It is."

"I mean, this was always you? Underneath?"

Sol nodded.

"I feel like I should slap you. This feels like the moment it would happen if this was a movie, you know?"

"You can if you'd like," Sol said, angling his head to the side.

"No, you'd probably like it. Besides, I'm not really mad. I understand why you did it. Why you've been hiding."

"I never wanted you to find out," Sol said.

"I wouldn't have believed it. Not without experiencing everything we've gone through or seeing all of this." Ginnie waved her hands around the room.

"Quite the sight, isn't it?"

Ginnie tried to smile. "You're not going to stay, are you?"

"I can't. Not like this."

She caressed Sol's human cheek. "You couldn't make another body?"

Sol stepped back and extended his claws. The spikes lining the undersides of his forelimbs retracted. The metallic sheen coloring his claws faded as the curved blades shriveled down to two doughy stumps. Sol groaned as human hands bloomed from the nubs and flexed their fingers.

Ginnie flinched as the digits suddenly retracted and long claws quickly snapped back into shape.

"I wish I could, but I'm afraid I'm all used up. I just don't have the energy to fuel another transformation." Sol shook his claws out. "The process would kill me. I'm no spring chicken, you know?"

Ginnie wiped a tear from her eye. "I'll miss you, Sol."

"Me too. At least I'll be able to take Charles forward before I go. He's ready. Look."

Ginnie turned around. There was a glowing light radiating behind Charles's head. Edgar brushed past her.

"What? What's everyone looking at?" Charles asked. He seemed suspended, trapped in the air—he tried to float backward, but stopped mid-flight. "I-I can't move."

"What's wrong with Opa?" Edgar asked. "His eyes just rolled back into his head!"

"Watch," Sol whispered.

CHAPTER 69
A NEW BODY

Edgar shielded his eyes as bright tentacles of light wriggled out from Opa's neck. The iridescent feelers thickened and grew longer, reaching for the floor.

Opa Chuck groaned as the muscles in his face spasmed. "It . . . it hurts," he said, squeezing his left eye shut. The corners of his lips drooped as his head rocked back and forth. Ghostly spume bubbled from his nose, drifted out, and evaporated.

"Oh, God! What's happening to him?" Edgar asked.

"Give it a moment," Sol said. "Despite appearances, your grandfather is in no danger."

The tentacles swayed in the air and wrapped themselves around each other, forming a glowing spinal cord. Veins of shimmering light raced into vertebrae and branched out in every direction.

"It looks like his nervous system," Clara whispered, pointing at the neural network knitting itself onto the air.

She was right. Edgar could see the faint outline of his grandfather's body as blue light coursed through the intricate pathways. The light flared and dimmed over and over again. But as the rhythm slowed, the blue luminescence faded into patches of dull yellow. The light faded completely and hardened into a plastery shell, enveloping his grandfather from the neck down.

Opa opened his eyes and groaned, "I can feel my body!"

The cast cracked as his arms and legs bent at their joints. Hands and fingers flexed free from their prison. Opa dug his fingers into his chest and pulled apart the plastery shell, sending clouds of yellow soot into the air.

As the dust settled, Opa Chuck stood marveling at his new body. He patted his arms, chest, and thighs as everyone looked on. The solidity was short lived, however, as Opa's head and body took on a familiar translucence.

Edgar stepped forward. "That's weird."

Opa Chuck raised an eyebrow. "What's that?"

"You're wearing a jogging suit. I thought you'd be naked for some strange reason."

Opa Chuck laughed. "Come here, you wonkadoodle!"

Edgar raced forward and hugged his grandfather for the first time. Light shimmered between them as they embraced. Gone was the rubbery texture of his grandfather's head. In its place was a sense of warmth he'd never felt while doing the Catch with just Opa's head. Edgar squeezed harder knowing that the feeling might not last.

Margaret stepped closer.

"Can I try?" she asked.

Edgar nodded.

Opa Chuck stood up and reached for his daughter. They smiled as their fingers interlaced. The Catch worked for his mother now too!

"Everyone! Group hug!" Edgar shouted.

Aunt Ginnie and Clara wrapped their arms around Opa Chuck. Edgar did the same and watched as his grandfather's eyes widened.

"No! No! No, not you, Sol!"

The professor scuttled backward and tucked in his arms.

Opa held up his palms. "No offense, but you're way too big . . . and those claws. Good, God!"

"None taken. I know that this body is a bit much."

Opa Chuck looked down at his ghostly form. "You know, I'm with Edgar on this. Why am I wearing clothes?"

Sol smiled. "Your mind created an image of what you looked like at the moment of your death. If you had died in the bath or in bed with a special—"

Opa Chuck raised his hands. "Ok, I get it. We get it."

A question bothering Edgar bubbled to the surface. It was always there and now he felt like he could get an answer.

"Professor, you know what I'd like to know?"

Sol shook his head. "What's that?"

"Why me? Why am I a Seer?"

Sol rubbed his claws together. "I've always believed Seers were nature's way of establishing balance, countering my kind's presence in your world."

"Ok, but of the billions of people on this planet, why was I born with these powers?" Edgar asked.

"Honestly, you probably have me to thank for that. I've lived in this area for the past forty years. Who knows how many times I crossed paths with your family. I drove past this street on my way to Ginevra's—"

"Oh, no!" Clara shouted.

Edgar turned. It was Opa Chuck. His grandfather's new body was evaporating. The outer edges of his shoulders and knees fizzled into plumes of white vapor.

Opa faced Sol. "What's happening to me?"

"My Gods, you're moving on. I didn't expect this to happen so fast."

"Where's Opa going?" Edgar asked. He scrambled to his grandfather's side and squeezed him by the waist.

"Into the afterlife. He's ready now," Sol said.

CHAPTER 70
SAYING GOODBYE

Edgar didn't care if his grandfather was ready. He wasn't.

But no matter how hard Edgar squeezed, Opa kept fading away. Not even joining hands with Clara stopped the process. If anything, their combined efforts seemed to quicken the evaporation. Their embrace passed through Opa without any resistance. Edgar stepped back and clutched his own head with both hands.

"There's not much we can do. Your grandfather is ready to move forward," Sol said.

Opa Chuck shook his head. "But I don't want to go."

"I'm afraid you don't have much of a choice. Your spirit is being pulled into the afterlife," Sol said. "If you don't say your goodbyes now, you'll never get the chance. The last thing your family will see is you fading into nothingness. Do you really want that?"

Opa stared at his transparent hands.

"This isn't fair!" Edgar said, clenching his fists. "We went through all of that just to lose Opa in the end. Isn't there anything we can do?"

Sol arched his head back and exhaled a stream of black smoke through his human mouth. The vapor pooled at the ceiling and floated down as a dark cloud. Veins of lightning streaked through the black mist.

"What is that?" Opa Chuck asked.

"A few extra minutes of time," Sol said as the cloud flattened itself into a dark screen. An image of a city made of iridescent glass appeared across the surface. Cobwebs of light crackled over the scene.

Opa Chuck placed a barely visible palm on the cloud. The strange lightning flowed into his skin and Opa's body slowly faded back into view.

"Charles, why don't you try giving your grandson a hug now," Sol said.

Edgar didn't wait. He sprinted forward and latched onto Opa's waist. This time, his arms didn't pass through.

"Please don't go," Edgar whispered. "I need you."

"I don't want to go, but Sol's right. I must be ready. I can feel myself being pulled away, even now," Opa Chuck said.

Edgar buried his face deeper into Opa's side.

Opa sighed. "What happens now, Sol? Do I disappear into thin air?"

Sol shook his head. He pointed at the strange cloud with his claw. "No, you'll walk through the portal into the other side. I'll be right behind to guide you on the journey, but you have to go now. Are you ready?"

"As I'll ever be," Opa said.

Sol stuck the tips of his claws into opposite corners of the black cloud and stretched the surface into a rectangle large enough for Opa to step through. He pinched one of the clay tablets and tossed it into the void.

Edgar flinched as sparks crackled in the darkness. The glass city faded in and out of view. Part of him wondered if this was the right thing to do.

"No, there's something wrong. I don't think—"

Someone squeezed his shoulder. It was his mother. "I know this is hard, honey, but look at your grandfather—he's ready."

Edgar glanced up and saw tears welling in his grandfather's eyes. His gaze was focused on that strange metropolis. A beatific smile stretched across his face.

"I'll be ok, kiddo. It's time for me to go. I can feel it." Charles kneeled and grabbed Edgar by the shoulders. "You've grown into a fine young man, and you have some wonderful people supporting you. I see a bright future ahead of you."

"I love you, Opa," Edgar said.

Opa tussled Edgar's hair. "I love you too."

Edgar wanted to scream. He didn't want a future without his grandfather. Every molecule in his body urged him to hold Opa back, but he knew that was impossible—the lower half of Opa's body was barely visible.

Opa stood and glided over to Margaret. He held her cheeks between his palms. "I'm so proud of you, Margie. You're an amazing mother."

Margaret wiped her eyes. "I wish we had more time. I'm going to miss you."

"Me too, kiddo. Me too."

As Opa Chuck turned to face Aunt Ginnie and Clara, his body from the waist down disappeared.

"I guess I'm running out of time," he said. "Thank you for protecting my family. And Clara, thank you for being such a great friend to Edgar."

"He's a good friend too, the best. I'm going to miss you too," Clara said.

Opa hovered closer to the professor.

"It's time," Sol said, extending a claw toward the portal.

Black tendrils of smoke wrapped around what was left of Opa's body and slowly guided him inside.

"I love you all," Opa Chuck said as he floated through. An iridescent glaze shimmered over the portal's surface and then turned black again.

Edgar sobbed into his hands. His mother, Aunt Ginnie, and Clara took turns trying to console him, but nothing they did or said could mend the crack in his heart. Opa was gone.

Sol said a few words to his mother, bowed, and stepped toward Edgar. His human mouth moved, but Edgar couldn't make out the words.

"What?" Edgar asked, rising from the floor.

"I said, it's been an honor, young man. You're the bravest Seer I've had the pleasure of meeting," Sol said, extending a claw.

He wanted to slap it away.

"So you were never a Seer, right?"

"No, but because I'm a Phantid, I had some of the same abilities and know what you can do." Sol clasped his claws together. "I know how much you loved your grandfather, Edgar, but it's better this way. You know that the Myrmidon would eventually come back for him.

"Was there really no way that Opa could have stayed?"

Sol shook his head. "I'm afraid not. I know this isn't easy for you. Give yourself some time to heal, ok?"

Edgar nodded. "I will. What about you? Where are you going?"

"Well, I can't go home just yet. Lugal made that clear, but there are a few worlds I can hide in while things sort themselves out back in Irkalla." Sol glanced at his walking cane on the floor. "Do me a favor and take care of that, will you? It's an antique."

Edgar picked up the monkey-headed blade and turned it in the air. He felt like a knight.

"It's a good look for you," Sol said, stepping toward the portal. His head swiveled on his neck stalk to face Aunt Ginnie. "Goodbye, my dear!"

Tendrils of black smoke swirled around Sol's body and slowly pulled him into the darkness.

"Wait!" Edgar yelled.

Sol wrenched half his body out to face Edgar. His claws clasped around the edges of the dark rectangle. Just past the professor's swept-back antennae, Edgar caught a glance of what looked like thousands of glowing balls orbiting the glass city.

"I have to know. Is Opa going to heaven now?"

Sol smiled and nodded as the mist pulled him through the portal.

ACKNOWLEDGMENTS

Sharing my stories is a dream come true and it's thanks to my family's endless support that I'm able to make this incredible gig possible.

I also want to thank the members of my critique group, the Weird Writers, for their feedback and encouragement.

Shout-outs to Robert P. Ottone, Kimberly Schebler, Victoria Navarra, Annie Sand, Andy Boyle, Yvonne Rao-Remy, Aven Lumi, Louise "Weezie" Prescott, Christina DeDora, Mandi Sabanos, and Michael Bonet.

High-fives, hugs, and endless gratitude to *Headhunters'* beta readers: Laura Lemke, Anthony Guido, Kerry Som, Brendan O'Grady, and Michael G. O'Connell.

And a huge thanks to the reader holding this book!

Tell your friends and loved ones about Edgar, Clara, and Aunt Ginnie's adventures. I hope to bring you many more deranged visions and nightmares in the near future!

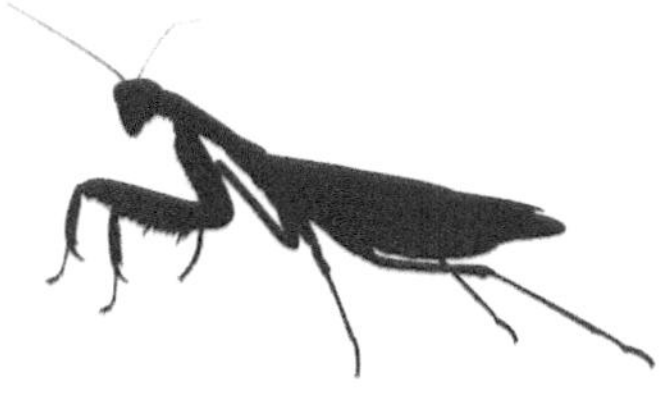

ABOUT THE AUTHOR

Luis Paredes is a speculative fiction writer and author of *Out On a Limb*, an urban noir fantasy. His genre-blending work appears in Tangled Web Magazine, the Kaidankai Horror Podcast, Crow & Cross Keys, Black Sheep: Unique Tales of Terror and Wonder, Max Blood's Mausoleum, and Tall Tale TV.

Fun fact: Luis's favorite animal is the platypus.

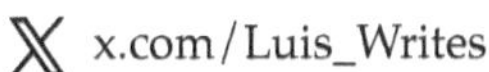

X x.com/Luis_Writes

instagram.com/luisparedeswrites

ALSO BY LUIS PAREDES

Out On A Limb

www.ingramcontent.com/pod-product-compliance
Lightning Source LLC
Chambersburg PA
CBHW022111310726
48972CB00007B/1986